ALIEN WARRIOR'S CAPTIVE BRIDE

JUNO WELLS

CONTENTS

1 / LONE SENTRY
LAROK

As Larok moved through the small shuttle, he inspected every single operating system, corrected every tiny mistake, and recorded every action he took. The queens didn't tolerate mistakes, and his queen was stricter than most. It was the reason his brethren were careful to avoid making her angry. Nothing good ever came of being noticed by a Draconian queen. Every being in the 'verse desired life, and lone sentinels like Larok were no different. Executing his duties perfectly was his best chance at staying alive.

Watchmen like him were chosen for their diligence, attention to detail, and ability to work alone for long periods of time. Larok was one of many such guards assigned to patrol the area just outside the mother ship's sensor range. If another ship encroached on their territory, their duty was to sound the alarm. Sentries like Larok were the first line of defense for the massive mothership.

Draconian queens were in constant conflict with one another, as legions of them fought over territory, planets, and riches. Thousands of ships roamed millions of parsecs of space, looking to assert their dominance. Warriors like him were thrown into battle on the whim of a queen. In an environment where only queens mattered, simple warriors were simply expendable.

Larok couldn't allow himself to be expendable, not now. He had a secret worth protecting. Sequestered deep in the underbelly of the mothership, his little hatchling sat safely concealed in the makeshift chamber his family had created. However, its shell would offer little in the way of protection if Queen Abraka discovered it.

Draconian queens were particular about whom they bred with. They were renowned for destroying any eggs they didn't fertilize themselves, and even their own if they suspected it of being less than perfect. Since she had not chosen him as a breeder, Abraka would not only destroy his little scion, but deal harshly with Larok and his family for attempting to conceal it from her.

That's how he ended up on this lonely assignment. It was the only way his sire could keep his breeding from being noticed on a ship packed with almost a thousand warriors. The older commander, Larok's father, was charged with managing security aboard the Draconian mother ship. The job of performing regular inspections of every shuttle fell to him and him alone. This had afforded his sire the opportunity to collect Larok's egg during an inspection ten cycles ago. Now, his unborn child was under the care and protection of his family.

That small shell, no larger than his fist, represented the continuation of his line as well as the risk of potentially wiping it out of existence, if Queen Abraka discovered their deceit. Still, what male would turn down an opportunity to pass down his genes? His little one was certainly worth everything his family was risking to ensure its survival.

Larok headed back to his tiny bridge and dropped into

his seat at the navigational panel. His fingers flew over the controls, as he carefully set the coordinates to move the shuttle to its next assigned position. Then he composed his daily report. He sent it along with a hope that all was well at home. Microns ticked slowly by, as he waited for his sire to acknowledge receiving his entry.

Moments later his communications relay crackled to life. "Greetings from the mothership of Queen Abraka, my hatchling. Your status report has been received, reviewed, and entered into the database."

Larok automatically responded with the standard return greeting. "Long live our illustrious queen."

"I'm afraid her time is near. Prepare yourself to be called home at a moment's notice."

"May I inquire after you and my fellow hatchmates?"

"I am well, as are your hatchmates. You have no cause to worry for any of your blood. I will speak with you soon."

Larok let out a sigh of relief when the com channel closed. His sire had communicated his little one and the rest of his small family was well. Glancing at his timepiece, he calculated that he had about three hundred microns to rest before it was time to repeat the process again. He set the automatic pilot and the proximity sensors, which would sound an alert if there was movement in his sensor range. He stood and stretched his tired muscles and headed to his quarters.

After peeling off his clothing, Larok stepped beneath the cleanser and allowed the fine warm mist to envelop his body. Pressing his hands against the wall, he thought about how lucky he was. Occasionally accidents happened. When all the planets were in proper alignment, and the goddess smiled on a male, magical things were possible. One such miracle happened when he'd been assigned to guard duty in the queen's chambers during a breeding cycle. He'd been stationed beneath one of the intake air vents. The unit had kicked on every nine microns for a full cycle, sucking air into the large vent as another unit across the room pumped fresh air. Though he hadn't realized it at the time, the room must have been thick with her pheromones, which washed over him with each intake of air. It was the only thing that could have ignited parthenogenesis.

Running his hand over his naked body, he slopped cleansing foam onto his skin. As far as males go, he was healthy, fit and in the prime of his life. His wings were as strong as any in the fleet. In addition, his line was gifted with other attributes he hoped had been passed on to his offspring.

It was a dangerous time to have a secret hatchling. Larok turned over the elder drone's new plan in his mind. Plotting against a queen was high treason. If their warriors had ever been that cunning, he could not remember reading about it in the ship's historical archives.

His mind swirled with all the new ideas he'd heard the elder drones talking about. They told tales of how several ships had escaped through a portal into another sector of space. It is said their brethren are free from the rule of vicious queens there. True freedom! The very idea was so different from anything he'd known that Larok could barely draw a picture of it in his mind's eye.

The alien queens on the other side of the rift were said to have beautiful smooth skin, soft strands growing from their head, and eyes that were all the colors of a nebula. The hardest part for him to fathom was the report that the alien queens befriended each other, had no desire for power, and rarely fought amongst themselves. Somehow the thought of touching a soft queen was alluring, but he'd learned long ago that queens were rarely what they seemed. Even if the wild tales were true, there was little chance of Larok's touching one of them. Since there were true breeders aplenty among his crew, no queen would think of a simple warrior with limited breeding ability as a consort.

Yet, it might still be possible for him to at least look upon an alien queen. The elders were busy concocting some plan to create an artificial rift when their queen died and escape to freedom, rather than yielding to a new Draconian Queen. It sounded dangerous and worried him greatly, for he now had a youngling to consider. Anxiety twisted in his gut. For his part, Larok preferred the danger of a queen he knew how to circumvent as opposed to one he knew nothing about.

No sooner had he gotten out of the cleansing unit than his proximity sensor shrieked. Shrugging into a fresh uniform and boots, he rushed back to his station to investigate. A subspace rupture filled his screen. He'd seen that happen from time to time. Since they usually dissipated before becoming large enough to cause an actual rift or pose a threat, he switched on the external image recorders and captured footage of the event. His queen would no doubt wish to see this with her own eyes.

As the microns clicked by, he realized the anomaly was not diminishing. Instead, it was growing in size and intensity. The thought occurred to him that he could fly right through the rupture and perhaps end up in the space his elders had spoken of. He kicked that idea out of his mind almost before the thought was fully formed in his head—Larok knew he would never leave his little one behind.

A brilliant white cavern opened as he watched, awestruck by its beauty, but also afraid, for it looked much like the mouth of a large celestial worm. A ship came flying through the vast round hole. The vessel was old and probably didn't have the necessary shielding to protect it from the gravitational pull of the anomaly. That must be why it was listing to one side and flying erratically. Unsure who it was or what they wanted, one thing was certain. They should not be encroaching upon his queen's territory. Arming his weapon, he decided to give the strange ship just enough of a jolt to send it back into its own sector of space.

ELLA SHRUGGED INDIFFERENTLY WITH ONE SHOULDER. "I never cared much for burgers, so once we lost most of the meat production facilities after the fall, I didn't really notice."

Hope stared wide eyed at her pretty blonde friend. "I would literally kill for a gourmet burger right now. Not a plain, old-fashioned fast food burger, mind, but a big, thick gourmet burger with the works."

Ella giggled, "I can't imagine you killing someone."

Riya wrapped her now dirty and tattered sari closer around her rail-thin form. "I miss panipuri. It's spicy, tangy, and sweet all at the same time." Looking around at a bunch of confused faces, she smiled brightly. "Think crispy dumpling but tasty rather than bland."

Hope rubbed her empty belly. "We need to stop. I was wrong. Talking about food is not just as good as eating it. In fact, chatting about all the delicious foods we miss from before the fall is just making me hungrier."

Ella's hands flew to her mouth. "We should talk about

which is the best of all of the alien species, since we're stuck with the squid men."

Riya moved closer. "We got it right the first time by signing on with the Taladar. They might have had strangely shaped heads, but they were really nice to us."

Hope said, "No, I think either the Strovian or Draconian guys. The Strovian are mostly big sexy warriors who like to show off for their women, and the dragon guys are hotties. You can only tell they have dragon DNA by the horns and wings."

Ella nodded her agreement. "I learned in my Alien Cultures class that they are all that remains of a once proud and prolific race of real dragons. They're supposed to be the watered-down version of a gigantic dragon in humanoid form."

A white-haired woman in a nearby cage, Marion, grabbed the bars and peered out to join the conversation. "I like the Nubians. I know everyone calls them fish heads, because they have a fin running over their scalp, but I think they're really handsome."

Hope laughed, "They don't even need human brides, Marion. Their species has tons of women."

Scratching her dirty scalp, she replied pensively. "Yeah, I know there's no shortage of Nubian women. Still that Nubian leader ended up with a nice older woman like me. What's his name? I can't seem to remember anything these days."

"It's because we're dehydrated. It messes with our ability to organize our thoughts." Ella's quiet voice always sounded logical, even under these extreme circumstances. Somehow just talking freely when they were alone helped them cope with the prolonged captivity.

Nodding, Marion continued advocating for the

Nubians. "The fact that he chose a mature bride makes me think they don't care about age so much."

Suddenly, their solitude was broken by the huge metal door unlocking. The metal-on-metal sound grated on everyone's nerves. Hope could tell because several women covered their ears. When the door slid open, what she saw on the other side was nothing short of nauseating.

Coming quickly to her feet, she gaped as did the other women in her cage. She was one of around a hundred women who'd signed up for the bride exchange program on Earth. After being traded to a little-known alien species known as the Taladar, their ship was raided by yet another race of aliens. She got the feeling the squid men didn't consider human women all that interesting, because they pulled them roughly off the Taladar ship and crammed them into a dozen or so large cages on their raiding ship. Quite honestly, she felt more like freight than a passenger.

Watching the slimy squid people approach, she heard Stephanie mutter under her breath. "What the hell do they want now? I've still got slime on me from their last little groping session."

Hope whispered, "Quiet. You know how they get when we whisper to one another."

"Screw them," her angry friend hissed back.

The alien that she was coming to think of as Head Squid Dude slithered into the room, leaving a thick, gray, malodorous slime trail in his wake. He looked a little ridiculous wearing nothing but a crude vest that hung loosely about his body. Though he was more humanoid than squid shaped, he did have eight tentacles in place of arms and legs. His shoulders were bumps on each side of his upper body, barely enough to keep his vest in place.

Several of his squid henchmen were bringing up the

rear. Why they wanted human women was a genuine mystery. They clearly weren't compatible with humans. A careful inspection verified they didn't seem to have sex organs at all. That didn't keep them from getting a little grabby, though. Being full-on groped was beyond creepy, but so far Hope had managed to escape that fate by keeping her head down and not making eye contact.

The plump squid bellied up to one of the cages containing much younger women. The small group looked to be in their mid-teens. Since they were too young to have been enrolled in the bride exchange, and they were brought in several days after the rest of the women, Hope figured they were probably abducted. She'd heard some muffled sobbing coming from that corner after lights-out, too.

The head honcho reached one slimy tentacle into the cage toward a young girl who promptly lost it. She froze, squeezed her eyes shut, and began mumbling *this is not happening* over and over again. Hope reacted without thinking. Grabbing the bars of her cage, she shouted. "Hey, you stupid, steaming pile of dog shit, that's just a baby! Pick on someone your own size!"

Stacy whispered, "Great going, Hope. Prepare to be slimed."

Ignoring her disgruntled friend, Hope watched the squid's reaction to being screamed at. Since he didn't actually have a head to turn, the alien's entire body reoriented to her direction, making a disgusting squishy sound. His body puffed up and at the center, it turned red, a dark, pulsing red. He began moving towards her. As most of the other women in her cage moved back, Hope wrapped her arms around her emaciated stomach and waited for the worst.

Why couldn't she ever keep her stupid gob shut? Her smart mouth and quick temper had gotten her into more trouble than she could shake a stick at, yet here she was, not learning her lesson all over again. Swallowing hard, she tried not to look as frightened as she felt.

Several women made small sounds of alarm. Only Ella and Stacy still stood at her side. "Step back. Don't be an idiot." Whispering to the brave pair only seemed to infuriate the squid more.

Watching him move was nothing short of terrifying, as he used his tentacles to grab onto the other cages and propel himself forward. His strength was unbelievable. The angry squid could probably tear her limb from limb if he had a mind to, and right now he looked like he was intent on doing just that.

Taking a staggering step back, she tried to avoid his grasp. Ella's arm locked through hers in a breathtaking act of defiance. Before Hope could even think of what to say to placate the angry alien, his moist feelers grasped onto the bars and he was jerking the huge cage violently as he spoke. What he was attempting to communicate was anyone's guess. Since none of them spoke Squid, all they could do was try to stay back and avoid eye contact. For some reason, their new alien captors hated being looked in the eye.

He reached through the bars to wrap one slippery tentacle around her arm. The tentacle was lined with small round suction cups made of some kind of spongy tissue. The harder he pulled the more tightly the suction cups gripped her. At some point, Hope realized they were burning round rings into her arm. Ella was trying with all her might to pull them apart, but the alien's grip was too strong.

Just when she didn't think she could stand it a second more, an alarm sounded through the communications system. Lighting around the edges of the ceiling began to blink. There was some kind of garbled information being spewed through the communicator clipped to Head Squid Dude's shoulder.

He deflated a bit and one tentacle floated over the scanning plate. It was hard to tell from his peculiar expression, but he seemed to be gloating about something. Yanking the cage open, he knocked Ella aside with very little effort. Stacy grabbed Hope around the waist and tried to pull her away from him. The angry squid yanked her out of Stacy's grasp and Hope was outside the cage before her two friends could mount a proper response. The squid was dragging her across the loading bay. The thick slime and the uneven surface made it impossible to keep her feet, and Hope stumbled, cracking one knee against the metal floor. Unable to see where they were going, she prayed it was just another cage.

They skidded to a stop in front of a capsule-shaped escape pod. Unsure whether to be terrified or relieved, she watched him pry it open. The horrible alien was extremely proficient with tentacles. The odd idea jumped into her mind that opposable thumbs were supposed to be the thing that enabled people to have fine motor skills. The squid jerked her forward, and she lost her train of thought. Just as he shoved her into the capsule-shaped pod, the entire ship shook.

That's when it occurred to her they were under attack. A sick feeling churned in the pit of her stomach when the glass door slid around and locked into place. They were under attack, and he chose this exact moment to launch her out in an escape pod. That couldn't possibly be a coincidence. She was clearly meant to be a distraction for whoever was firing at their ship.

Beating the glass front of the pod, she screamed for him

to open it back up. The self-satisfied expression on the squid's face told her that wasn't going to happen. The boss man was solving several problems at once by sending her out. He was getting rid of his troublemaker, teaching the other women what would happen if they didn't fall into line, and using a valuable human female as a distraction in order to make a clean getaway. Yep, Head Squid Dude was anything but stupid.

Suddenly, Hope felt the ground fall out from under her. The sensation of falling gave way to one of being propelled down at an accelerated rate. A mask dropped from the ceiling, and she put it over her face. It wasn't shaped for a human face, but oxygen was pouring out of it, so she breathed it in. The sight of metal was replaced by complete darkness accompanied by the twinkling of stars in the distance. Her knees buckled and she slid down to the floor, banging her already bruised knee. Since the pod was standing room only, she felt a bit like a cork in a bottle.

Hot tears poured down her face, as she realized life as she knew it was over. Whoever was shooting at the raiders might not even want a human. What if she got caught in the crossfire? What if the other ship ignored her? What if she was left floating through space for all eternity? Worse yet, what if the raider decided to destroy her pod in a blaze of glory? Exploding things were more distracting than floating things after all.

Forgetting to keep the mask over her face was a mistake that she realized all too late. Blackness clouded her vision, even as she tried to stand up to reach the mask.

3 / RESCUING A QUEEN

LAROK

CURSING UNDER HIS BREATH, LAROK LAUNCHED everything his small shuttle had in the way of weapons at the alien ship. Nothing worked, and the interloper slipped through just as the portal was closing. A growl of frustration escaped from the back of his throat, as Larok geared up to pursue the vessel. That's when he noticed something hurtling through space. They'd launched an escape pod. Excitement flooded his system as it occurred to him the alien ship's captain might be looking for an escape. Instead of pursuing the alien vessel, he made directly for the life pod.

The moment his shuttle came into range, he scanned it. His warrior training meant that Larok knew things weren't always what they seemed. It might be a decoy meant to draw his attention from battle. There was every possibility the pod could contain an explosive device or some type of biological contaminant. When the scan revealed only the body of one alien queen, he immediately used a grappling arm to pull it into his rear loading bay. He rushed back to tend to the alien queen with his blood hammering through his veins. Who in their right mind would risk the life of one of their queens to create a diversion? It must be a being with a devious and evil mind.

Larok carefully rolled the round pod over and unsealed the glass door. Looking down at her, his mouth went dry. She was small, smooth, and soft. The small strands growing from her head were the color of fire. Tiny matching spots dotted her delicate face. It felt like time stood still for a brief moment before it sped up to something approaching the speed of light. This pale creature looked much like they described the alien queens from a faraway sector of space. The truth of the situation powered through his brain as he put the pieces of the puzzle together. Of course she did, they were the only aliens using wormholes that he knew of.

He lifted her small body from the pod and carried her to a nearby bench. Having an alien female was going to change everything for his people. The last bout of breeding had taken a lot from their harsh Draconian queen. She was dying, and every warrior knew it. How outrageously lucky that an alien queen wandered into their midst just when they needed her the most. The other ship had gotten away, but it mattered little in face of the rare treasure in his arms.

He seized a medical scanner and then moved it over her frail body. Though such devices were limited, from what it could tell him, she seemed well. Larok found odd round burns on the inside of one arm. Whatever the sticky substance they spread over the wounds in an attempt to heal her seemed to be exacerbating the lesions. He tore some cleansing wipes from a small container and cleaned her wounds before carefully closing each one with a dermal healing unit. She was tiny, weak and dirty. The scanner indicated she was also severely dehydrated. Larok growled his frustration, thinking how much he'd love just a few minutes alone with whatever being did this to her.

Before he could get fluids into her, she sat up abruptly. Her clear green eyes were very different from the dark eyes of his people. Scooting back, he realized he was gaping at her in a most inappropriate manner. She grabbed his uniform, yanking him forward. The words coming from her mouth were strange. They seemed to be commands of some type. Never one to disobey a queen, his mind raced to figure out the best course of action. Since her language was not in their programs, he voice prompted the language processor to capture enough of her speech to establish a root language.

After breaking her grasp on his uniform—she was strong for such a little thing—he grabbed an electronic touch pad and turned it on to a drawing program. It was crude to expect a queen to communicate this way, but until the language processor completed its cycle, there was little else he could do.

She was quick to use the pad. Drawing an image of a ship with the tip of her finger, she frowned and began drawing multiple squares in one area. Drawing a line from one the squares, she sketched out what appeared to be a detention box. Larok could tell because of the long bars spaced close together. His mouth fell open when she began to sketch out others of her kind in the box. Though her images were rough, he recognized they were others like her because she drew a few of the long filaments growing from their heads. She pointed from herself to the people in the boxes.

Shock tore through him as he realized she had admitted to being a criminal. It had never once occurred to him to think that queens could be criminals. She kept pointing to the ship she'd drawn and then out the only portal in the room. Unless he missed his guess, she was telling him to take her back to the ship where she'd been detained. At least she was a criminal agreeable to serving out her sentence. That earned her genuine respect in his eyes.

Nodding his agreement, he headed back to his station. She followed behind him, when it was clear that she should have stayed to rest. He could have easily gestured that suggestion to her. Since warriors were not permitted to give directions to queens, even ones guilty of a crime, he refrained from making his thoughts on the matter known.

He gently moved her into the second seat and strapped her safely into place. No warrior worth his wings would fail to ensure the safety of a queen. Dropping into the pilot's seat, he knew better than to let a discovery like this go unreported.

Once again, his fingers flew over the console opening a line. He made a tiny chirping noise and then immediately shut the line back down on his end. He turned on his scanners and tried to determine which direction the prison ship had taken as he waited for his sire to find a secure line and signal him back. Within moments his communication system alerted him to an incoming message.

"What occasions a clandestine conversation, my hatchling?"

"A Wormhole opened in space and a ship came through."

"Tell me you fired on the vessel and destroyed it."

"I fired, but I was forced to break off pursuit in order to secure an escape pod. I believe it was launched to distract me long enough for the ship to escape."

His sire sighed, "Continue."

"I retrieved the escape pod and discovered it contained

a small alien queen with fire-colored strands growing out of her head."

Larok heard his father gasp, and quieter gasps from his siblings in the background. "You have possession of alien queen?"

"She communicated that she is a criminal and wishes to be returned to the prison ship."

"Don't be absurd. It is impossible for a queen to be a criminal, for they can do no wrong."

"What do you wish me to do with her, my sire?"

"Bring her to the mother ship. I will cue your brethren to provide an escort. Queens are precious. I'll risk no harm to the one who has come into our care."

"Understood, my sire."

"You know to slip in through the underbelly of the ship."

"I do. Using the regular loading bays would alert Queen Abraka."

"Our queen is not well enough to battle, but she would send warriors to do her dirty work."

"No one will see our boarding father. You have my word."

His sire's voice relaxed. "You have served with honor today, my scion."

At his sire's kind words, Larok's chest swelled and his eyes prickled. Being recognized for outstanding service was such a rarity, Larok was caught off guard. He choked back his emotions before saying, "Meet us in approximately fifty microns and see the alien queen for yourself. You will not be disappointed."

"I will bring all the elders. Take care, my scion."

Shutting off the com, Larok entered the correct coordinates.

The small queen coughed and he instantly remembered she was dehydrated. Reaching under his console, he pulled out a hydration packet and a food ration bar. Opening each, he offered them to the weakened queen. Her trembling hand took the items and she motioned for him to take her away in pursuit of the alien vessel.

It felt awful to deceive their new queen, but without knowing the words of her tongue, there was little he could do at the moment to explain they were not returning her to the prison ship. Clicking quickly through the engine initiation sequence, he maneuvered the ship around and headed for the mother ship.

The moment the ship began moving, the alien queen relaxed and began nibbling from the food bar. Larok tried not to stare at her but it was difficult to refrain from sneaking peeks.

She leaned over, broke off a piece of the food bar, and held it out to him. When he opened his mouth to speak, her small hand darted out, and she dropped the piece in his mouth. Queens do not feed warriors. Perhaps the small criminal queen was also mentally unbalanced. He quickly chewed the bite and held up his hand when she tried to give him a drink of her hydration fluid. She insisted, so he took a quick sip to make her happy. He must have pleased her because her facial expression changed.

She showed all her teeth to him. They were very white and rather than being sharp like a regular person, they were blunted. Unwilling to misstep, he made the mating gesture back to her. It felt awkward to be approached by an alien queen for mating so soon after meeting. It was something he never thought to experience in his lifetime. He only knew how to return the mating gesture because he'd read it in a well-worn book, secretly, when all his siblings were asleep.

She spoke again. Touching her chest, she said, "Ho-pe." She reached out and she touched his chest. The queen touched him, touched him on purpose. The questioning look on her face made him rack his brain for the correct response. She tapped his chest again. "Dra-con-i-an"

Suddenly, he got excited. Nodding he pronounced his species correctly. "Draconian."

She nodded and touched her chest again. "Ho-pe. Hom-on."

Her language had a lot of the hissing sound, making difficult to pronounce. She repeated herself several times before he realized she was obviously asking his name. This is why simple warriors were not companions for queens. They lacked the intelligence for such duties. He articulated his name clearly. "Lar-ok. Draconian."

She tested his name on her tongue several times, and then made the mating gesture again by showing all her teeth. Once again he reluctantly returned the gesture, secretly wishing the language program would complete its task. The diminutive queen seemed happy to chatter on and on. The more she talked, the more she seemed to relax. This was good because the more she spoke, the quicker the program would unlock the secrets of her language. He encouraged her the best he could to continue speaking. It was hard to turn away when she began waving her arms around in a peculiar fashion. There was something strangely compelling about this small queen and her animated ways, but he couldn't figure out quite what it was.

HOPE

Wiggling her arms like tentacles, Hope continued trying to make him understand her plight. "They've got like eight arms, eight legs, and ooze slime. I hate to say this, but they're totally gross."

The bulky warrior nodded as he worked the controls, making her think he was open to hearing all about her ordeal.

Making an open and close gesture with the fingers on one hand, she leaned forward and pressed the tips of her fingers against his arm. "Each tentacle has dozens of little round suckers that burn like hell when one of them grabs you. That's not even the worst thing about getting mauled by the slimy creatures. It's the slimy stuff the suckers exude that's the real problem. It feels like acid or something." Rubbing her hand over the area that had been affected, she found it smooth. "I've never felt anything like it before, and I hope I never do again."

He pointed to the inside of her arm, and she turned her arm over to look at the area where she'd been injured. She observed the milky-white skin was smooth and clear. Grinning at him, she exclaimed, "I don't know what you did there, but it fixed me right up. My friend Stacy got suctioned, and it took days for the marks to fade. You must have some super-good medicine on your cute little ship."

Gesturing around with one hand, she continued. "Or is this considered a shuttle? I don't know much about spaceships or space, except what I've seen on the holo vids playing in the marketplace." Letting her eyes roam over the handsome warrior, she couldn't conceal her delight at being rescued by a Draconian warrior. "That's how I knew you were a Draconian."

Upon hearing his species mentioned, his head whipped around to look at her and his strange pliable horns-like things shifted slightly. There were oval slits on each upturned end. The one closest to her flared in similar fashion to a nostril. It gave the perception of him sensing the air in her direction. "I'm damn lucky to get picked up by one of the good guys. I think it's really cool that you're the only alien species that doesn't pay or trade for brides." Rolling her eyes, she quipped. "Then again, why would you need to? You're all so gosh-darn good-looking. What with the pretty designs on your skin, crazy horns, and those brooding dark eyes, I'll bet every woman who ever set eyes on you couldn't get enough. I have to say, the wings are much more impressive in person than on the holo vids. Damn, dude, your wingspan must be ten or twelve feet!"

Sitting back in her chair, she couldn't keep the smile off her face for anything. "Once we rescue all the other women, I want to visit your home world. I saw Queen Cassandra on the holo videos. She's got the most adorable little Draconian babies. They have the most delicate wings, but somehow they manage to fly with them. They say that hot husband of hers never leaves her side, even for a minute. That's about the most romantic thing ever, don't you think?"

Her handsome rescuer only grunted. A light giggle spilled out before Hope could help herself. Being rescued from slimy alien asshats, by the galaxy's most honorable race of aliens was clearly making her giddy. This was the best possible outcome that could have happened.

"I always talk too much when I'm nervous. You're easy to talk to, because you can't understand a flipping word I'm saying, can you, handsome?"

He made some kind of cute chirping sound and went back to flying the ship.

"You know something? I don't even care that you can't understand what I'm saying. You're gonna help me rescue the other women, so who gives a flying fig?"

Stuffing the last bit of food bar in his mouth, she grinned. "Thanks for the rescue and for sharing your food with me. The stuff they were feeding us on the squid ship tasted like dog food. Not that we have dogs on Earth anymore, but I still remember what their food smelled like, because I had a poodle when I was growing up. I wish you could have met Paws. He was the nicest pet in the entire world."

Suddenly a computerized voice came over the ship's com. "You named your pet after a body part?"

Jolting forward, she had a hard time tamping down her excitement. "You can understand me now?"

"My computer had to process your language."

Sure enough, the shuttle's computer was translating what they were saying after each of them spoke.

"Thank God. I was getting tired of talking to myself."

"It is fortunate that you like to talk. The computer

required large fragments of speech in order to sort out the rudiments of your language."

"All right, I have two things to say. First, thanks for pulling me out of that life pod. I was getting claustrophobic and panicking about being stranded in space. Second, thank you for helping me free the other women."

"There are more criminals like you aboard the alien vessel?"

Her excitement came to a hard stop, as she gaped at him. "I'm not a criminal. What in the 'verse would make you think that?"

"My apologies, Queen Hope. You drew images of people behind bars and pointed to yourself."

Her expression smoothed out. "I see how you might have come to that conclusion. We aren't criminals. We were supposed to be brides for the Taladar elite. Unfortunately, our ship got raided. The slimy tentacle men stole all of us and the cargo, and then blew up the Taladar ship. It's a shame too, because the Taladar were really sweet guys."

His horns flattened down on each side of his head. "Gods of chaos, you were a hostage?"

Nodding, she took a deep breath. "Everyone knows how honorable Draconian warriors are. I'm lucky to get picked up by you." Smoothing back her wild red hair, she lifted her chin. "Clearly not every alien in the galaxy is as trustworthy as your people."

Staring at her, the warrior seemed pensive. When he didn't respond, a stilted silence spun out between the two of them.

Uncomfortable with the awkward stillness, Hope began talking again. "I actually studied up on all the alien peoples before I signed up for the bride's registry. Draconians were my first choice but you were all too far away for me to get to your ship."

"I honestly have no idea what you're talking about."

"I'm talking about Queen Cassandra inviting every woman to settle on your new home world."

"Our queen is Abraka. She is coming to the end of her time, and she has no tolerance for other queens in her territory."

"What do you mean by that?"

"She is an older queen and nearing the final phase of her life. Still, she would not want you in her territory."

"Abraka? That's an unusual name for a human woman."

"Clearly, our queen is Draconian."

Shaking her head, Hope dismissed his response out of hand. "You know there are no *Draconian* queens in the Naxis! Only human."

"What is the Naxis?"

"The Naxis is our sector of space. You know, the nexus where three galaxies meet? It encompasses about fifty habitable worlds that are all are joined together in an Intergalactic Council of Planets. How can you not know that?"

"Our sector of space is called Exion, Queen Hope."

"I've heard that name before. It's the area Draconians come from, not where you are now."

"Again, I do not know of what you speak. In our galaxy there is no council of planets. There is nothing but Draconian queens, and none go by the strange name of Cassandra."

"What are their names?"

"Abraka, Hevela, Darela, Laraka..."

"Stop. Those are not human names."

"Correct. They are not human names because they are

not human queens. The ship that brought you here created a wormhole into our sector of space. You are..."

"Oh hell no. I am not trapped on the dark side. Tell me I'm not."

"I do not know what the dark side is, tiny queen."

"It's what we call the sector of space where the Draconian queens control everyone and everything, or what you call Exion."

"I am sorry, but you are in the Exion galaxy, and the queens do rule just as you say."

"Turn this spaceship right around and take me back."

"The wormhole closed behind the ship carrying your fellow queens, trapping all of you in our sector. I have not the capacity to open a wormhole. This is a shuttle, not a mother ship. Even our best scientists have not yet perfected wormhole travel."

Unsnapping her safety harness, Hope sprang to her feet. Pressing her palms over her eyes, she paced back and forth mumbling to herself. "I've just jumped out of the frying pan and into the fire." Walking up to a wall of the cramped room, she leaned her forehead against it, bumping it softly a few times. "I'm not safe here. The Draconian queens are all crazy. They'll tear me apart." Spinning on her heel to look at the nice warrior who rescued her, she spoke. "I saw the footage of a fight between one of your Draconian queens and human women. It took a lot of women to bring that queen down."

The warrior startled in his seat. "Then it's true what they say. On the other side of the wormhole, we are free."

Nodding, Hope murmured, "Your new home world is amazing. It got voted into the Intergalactic Council almost immediately."

A light lit up on his control panel, and Larok

murmured, "Hold on, Queen Hope. I am locking my top port to a docking ring on the mother ship."

Grabbing a metal bar running along the side of the wall, Hope felt herself going numb. "You're not my rescuer are you? You're taking me to be killed by your queen."

The shocked warrior shook his head vehemently. "You will be protected at all costs. I've told you that our queen is weak and dying. We will keep your arrival secret."

"What of the other women?"

Turning back to his controls Larok responded quietly. "I am but a simple warrior. Do not ask me questions of import, for I have no answers to give you, my frightened queen."

"I understand. I've got no right to make demands of you."

The shuttle jerked as he locked it to the docking ring. A large hole opened in the ceiling and a metal ladder slid down. Larok moved it into a secure position and held out his hand to assist her up the first few steps.

Forcing her feet to move, she looked up into the brightly lit opening. Taking the step that closed the distance between them, Hope wrapped her arms around him. "Whatever happens, I want to thank you for saving me from the raiders."

His arms came up around her. For once in her miserable life, Hope felt safe and protected. No matter how strong she usually was on the outside, her anxieties and self-doubt thrived inside. Even those, for once, fell still under his gentle touch. She felt him nuzzle his face into her hair, as he whispered words too faint for the computer to pick up.

LAROK

GOING STILL IN HER ARMS, LAROK'S MIND WAS flooded with a thousand new ideas. Up until this moment he had thought his life would be filled with hard work and duty. He'd seen himself as a sentinel, a warrior, and just recently, sire to his own small hatchling. Never had the idea of being a breeder to soft luxurious queen entered his mind. Yet, here he was being embraced by the talkative little alien queen. She'd bared her blunt little teeth at him, and shockingly enough he'd reciprocated the mating gesture.

Without willing them to, his arms came up around her. Pulling her close, he inhaled the scent of the long filaments growing from her head. She smelled like the filth of her captivity, but his keen sense of smell delved beneath that stench to take in her purely feminine scent. It was light, sweet, and thoroughly intoxicating. Digging his fingers into her soft body without meaning to, he reveled in how good she felt in his arms.

For her part, the small queen trembled slightly and clung to him more tightly. She was clearly terrified about being caught in the Exion expanse of space and facing all the dangers of the unknown. "Fear not, my precious queen. I will allow no harm to come to you."

Unsure if she understood his words or took strength from his embrace, he allowed her to slip from his arms. She hauled in a deep breath, as she stood staring up at the docking port. Slowly she stepped up to the ladder and began making her way up. His brethren helped her up the final couple of steps.

Rushing back to the console Larok tore out the data chip. It contained all the information his shuttle recorded during his latest deployment. Staring down at the small clear flexible chip, he realized it also held the key to his people communicating with their new queen. Priority number one was to protect his new queen, but getting her language elements embedded in a neural download was critical as well. His brethren would need that to communicate effectively with her. It was not helpful to have a queen if one could not readily understand her commands. Luckily her language seemed to be built off an ancient root language they had assimilated long ago, otherwise it would have taken the computer much longer to formulate a translation matrix.

The sound of her voice calling him pulled Larok from his internal thoughts. He hurried to catch up with his new queen. He found Queen Hope was blinking, and holding her hands up to shield her eyes. Clearly her human eyes took longer to adjust to the brighter lights of the mother ship's loading bay.

Larok stepped to his queen's side and wrapped a wing protectively around her small body. Pride surged in his chest when she moved closer to him. His father's gaze bespoke his pride in Larok securing the approval of their new queen so quickly.

Reaching out one hand, Larok held out the data crystal

in the palm of his hand. "In addition to the usual data on this deployment, it has her language encryption on it.

His sire spoke. "Create a neural download immediately. Our new queen will be anxious until she can speak freely to us." One of the older men nodded. Snatching the data chip from his hand, the elder warrior rushed over to a console and began processing the information.

Larok looked around at perhaps twenty older warriors. They were all staring curiously at his new queen. Rather than curious, Queen Hope seemed overwrought to the point of panicking. She burrowed down under his wing and wrapped both arms around his waist. Enfolding her in a warm embrace, he ran his hand up and down her back. "Fear not, my queen. You are among friends."

Once again his father spoke. "She cleaves to you, my scion."

"I am chosen. She voiced her gratitude to me for rescuing her and demonstrated the mating gesture to me rather emphatically on more than one occasion. I have no idea if we are breeding-compatible with the humon species, but I submit to her authority in this matter."

Elder Thermon spoke. "I believe they pronounce the word as human. It is a rare gift you bring to your brethren this day, scion of Jeron."

Looking down into her beautiful eyes, Larok whispered. "She is unlike the queens we have known."

Casting a warm glance in the human queen's direction, Elder Thermon murmured, "Clearly what you say is true. She is small, frightened and weak. Yet, I sense a kindness and raw sensual beauty we have never encountered in an alien queen."

Seeking to steer the elder warrior away from her physical attributes, Larok responded diplomatically. "She was abducted and harmed. I believe that once she gets her bearings, we will see a different side of my new queen."

Jeron spoke, "I have no doubt that is true."

Thankful for his sire's support, Larok relaxed a tiny bit.

HOPE

Swallowing thickly, Hope looked around the room. It was full of warriors, and they were all down on one knee, with both arms crossed over their chest. Every single one had bowed his head submissively. It looked like a sea of horns, all drooping in submission. It was a bizarre pose, and it was super weird to see them all doing it at the same time.

"What's going on here?" Growing more uncomfortable by the second, she saw their heads come up when she spoke. Gesturing, she encouraged, "You shouldn't be down on the cold metal floor that way. Stand up." Looking back down in the hole she stated a little louder, "Larok, where are you? Time to get your handsome ass on up here, cause I've got no idea what I've stumbled into."

Her throat tightened up, when the warriors all stood. They were larger than she thought at first and having them towering over her at such close proximity was kind of intimidating.

Willing herself to get with the program, she looked over the crowd. A couple of the warriors were like Larok. They had his coloring, and the design of their wings was extremely similar. The rest were a mixed bag. They had different wings and starkly diverse coloring. Though none had hair, they seemed to be different around the ears and in height. There were a couple of unifying features, such as hauntingly beautiful dark eyes and flexible horns.

Though she didn't sense any hostility from them, Hope still felt a little off-balance and vulnerable, being in a room with so many males she didn't know. The fact that she was on the wrong side of the divide between worlds, and her safety was anyone's guess only added to her anxiety. What had at first seemed like such good fortune was turning into a surreal experience. Thankfully, Larok climbed out of the hole and wrapped one gigantic wing securely around her waist. Turning to get a good look at the wing, she found it was jointed and its blue skin was baby soft.

As he spoke in muted tones with the other warriors in their native language, everyone's attention was drawn away from her for the moment. A small voice whispered from the deep recesses of her mind, urging her to run. Thankfully, the more logical side of her brain prevailed. Running wasn't an option when there's nowhere to run. Besides it would just make her seem stranger than she probably already seemed to the taciturn bunch of warriors.

Hope moved closer to the warrior who had rescued her, resting her head on his shoulder. The distracted warrior responded by instinctively wrapping his other arm around her. Glancing up at him, she chewed her lower lip as she watched the expressions moving across his face. He had a strong jaw, and a design inked down the side of his neck. Reaching up, she ran her finger down the markings. It seemed almost utilitarian, rather than ornamental. His hand came up and covered hers tenderly.

It hit her hard and fast that the earnest warrior standing

protectively at her side was her rock in a sea of turbulence, the only element she halfway understood or trusted at the moment. His firm hold on her was a grounding force, one she desperately needed.

The older warrior who'd been working at the console rushed back to their side with a weapon in his hand. Without conscious thought she quickly moved to Larok's other side, putting as much distance as possible between herself and the armed stranger. Everyone seemed taken aback. Larok held up an arm to keep the warrior away from her. Holding out his hand, he waited for the other man to drop the weapon into his hand.

To her absolute shock he brought the weapon up to the side of her neck, right below her ear. His other arm was gripping her too tightly for her to have any chance of getting away. Murmuring something in a low whisper, Larok pulled the trigger twice. At first Hope thought it was some kind of energy weapon designed to scramble her thought processes. That wasn't quite true. Though she was mortified, her brain was still working properly, or as properly as could be expected under such extreme circumstances.

She watched as the aliens loaded the weapon over and over again, taking turns shooting the fatty tissue right under their ear. Strangely enough, each warrior only got one shot instead of two.

Something loosened in her chest. It must be a vaccine or something of that nature. Her ears slowly filled with words. Glancing around, she saw Larok's mouth moving. "Fear not my queen. You are safe among our people. You must relax and let the language program graph onto your neural tissue."

Excitement and relief flooded her body. "I can understand you!" Shaking her head in disbelief, she placed her hand over her wildly beating heart as it slowed to steady thump. Sweet day in the morning, she really needed to calm the heck down and stop thinking the worst in every situation.

Larok smiled down at her. "We can understand your words as well."

"That's great and all, but I gotta ask if there is anything at all we can do to save my friends." It was probably wrong to start asking for favors right off the bat, but Hope had no intention of allowing that raider to get away with a cargo of stolen women.

The older warrior who looked most like Larok spoke. "There are more of your kind in our space? Your protectors were not..."

Larok broke in, "They are not males assigned to protect her. My queen refers to her friend queens. They are being held hostage on the ship that launched her escape pod."

Chirps of alarm sounded off around her. "How many friend queens are in danger?"

Seeing her opportunity, Hope jumped right into the conversation feet first. "There are almost a hundred of us. We were crammed in cages in their cargo bay. They fed us disgusting food and almost no water."

The older man's face contorted into a mask of fury and his horns jerked to into a standing position. "Who? Tell me who would dare treat a queen in such a way?"

Hope launched into the whole explanation about the squid guys and their sucker lined tentacles. By the time she finished her tirade they were all gaping at her. One of the men stated darkly. "You are a queen, so what you say must be true. I cannot draw the image of ten times ten queens all being abused in such a way."

"Well you better believe it, cause that's just what's

happening." Taking a deep breath, she did the most coun-
terintuitive thing she could think of. "I want to meet with
your queen."

Larok immediately spoke. "She will kill you."

"I know they're all crazy because of the parasites but..."

Larok spoke. "We do not know of what you speak, my
queen. Please explain."

"You know, the parasites?"

"We do not know."

"Queen Cassandra created a public service announcement and distributed it to all member worlds explaining the
Draconian situation."

Several of the elder warriors sounded off one after
another.

"What's a member world?"

"Is a public service announcement similar to writ of
compliance?"

"Draconians do not have a *situation*." The last warrior
spoke with a quiet dignity.

Looking from man to man, she realized they honestly had
no idea what she was banging on about. Before she could get
turned around to explain further, Larok scooped her up into
his arms and began walking off with her. "I am taking my
new queen to the medical bay on this level. She can answer
your questions while our healers perform a health scan."

Giving him a nice hard thump on the chest, Hope
frowned up at him. "I can walk. Put me down."

"I am your chosen protector. As such, it is my duty to
see to your safety. It is the one and only situation in which a
warrior may assert authority over a queen."

When he clutched her tighter, Hope realized he was
serious about carrying her the entire way for no apparent

reason whatsoever. "Fine, but it's not going to keep me from talking."

Almost smiling, he replied sincerely. "I never for single micron thought it would, my queen."

"What's a micron?"

"A micron is measurement of time known throughout the galaxy. It has been a little over a micron since I picked you up."

"You're really smart, aren't you?" Looking up at his handsome face, she murmured. "And you have pretty eyes." He smiled, showing all his teeth again. "And really sharp teeth."

Several amused chirps sounded around them. Larok pulled her tighter against his chest. "Now is not the time for courting, my queen. There will be time enough for that once your friend queens are secured, and their tormentors are dealt the justice they so richly deserve."

"I wasn't flirting." Though she was trying for indignant, her voice came out as breathy.

"You were."

"I was not."

"I am but a warrior. It is not my place to argue with a queen."

Staring into his eyes, she knew telling a guy he had pretty eyes was kind of flirting. Now she'd discovered that telling a warrior he had sharp teeth must also be considered flirtatious among his kind. Unable to keep the smile off her face, she admitted. "Maybe I was flirting a little. You're hot, and I'm pretty stressed. Now is not the best time to be flirting, you're probably right about that much."

Sitting her down on a hovering exam table, he tilted her face up so he could look into her eyes. "You are very different from the queens we have known. No Draconian queen would give quarter to a warrior so easily."

"Thankfully, my bitchy gene is a recessive one."

"I have no idea what that means."

Getting lost in his interested gaze, she responded teasingly. "It means I really like you, and not just because you rescued me."

Larok leaned low, to her low height on the table, to run his face down one side of hers and back up the other side. "All that I am, I offer to you."

Grinning at his formal flirtation, she quipped, "I'm not quite stupid enough to pass up an opportunity like that. Whatever it is you're offering, I'm definitely interested in having."

HOPE

A WARRIOR WEARING A GREEN UNIFORM FLUTTERED his wings. It seemed to be the socially acceptable way of interrupting their intimate moment, the Draconian version of clearing his throat. "Sorry to intrude, my queen. I am the Healer Kalar. If you explain the problem you are having with your recessive genome, I will do my best to repair the damage."

Glancing up at the accommodating male, Hope couldn't help but laugh. "Oh sweetheart, I was just joking about that. I guess I'm not quite as funny as I think I am."

Worry creased the brows of the multitude of elder warriors squeezing into the tight space. "It makes sense that you all want to check me over, since I'm an alien and all. Unlike your queen, I don't have any parasites or *anything* like that." Holding up two fingers, she added, "Scout's honor."

Larok stepped back, as Kalar turned on a medical scanner. "What makes you think our queen has a parasite?"

"Because all your queens do."

The healer spoke without looking up from his screen. "I do not believe that is accurate information."

"Queen Cassandra made a public service announcement—we saw it on my home planet. She showed us that every queen gets one whether she wants it or not. It's some kind of vicious organism that gets implanted in their stomach cavity. They only allow enough queens to be born to serve as hosts."

"That is simply not true."

"It is! She showed a young queen and the parasite they'd removed from her gut. She was real sweet. Queen Cassandra said the parasite enters her body during a special coming of age ceremony. The woman enters the cave of knowledge, walks through some pool of glowing water, and comes out infected."

"That is the sacred rite of ascension." Larok seemed to understand almost the moment the words left his mouth. "If what you say is true, the parasite is the one ascending."

"It's all true. I was both fascinated and creeped out by the announcement, so I paid attention to all the details."

When no one responded, she continued. "After it roots into the woman's body, the creature controls her mind. They made it real clear that they can infect other women with their young. They live to propagate and are really hard to exterminate."

"You lie."

Maybe she shouldn't have used the word exterminate when speaking to aliens. It was kind of harsh. Unfortunately, it was also too late to do anything about that, now that she had stuck her foot into her mouth in the worst way imaginable. Hope prudently elected to modulate her voice. "Why would I lie?"

The healer seemed even more perturbed than the other shocked warriors. "What you say is impossible."

"Look, I might be wrong or mistaken about what I saw in the announcement. But I would never lie."

Several of the warriors began to panic slightly. "My queen may be ruthless as are all queens, but she is Draconian."

"The young queen that got rescued spoke in the announcement. She cautioned everyone to be on the lookout for signs of infection. She said no female has left their home world without ascending in ten thousand years."

Kalar's hand came out hard and fast around her throat. "Your lies will not turn us from our queens, human."

Before she could respond, Larok had a weapon—Hope thought it was a laser pistol—digging into Kalar's chest. "Take your hands off my queen, Kalar. You have no right to lay hands on a queen in such a way. The punishment for harming a queen is death. You know this, my friend."

Shoving the healer's hands away, Hope tried to dial down the danger by offering the only suggestion that came to mind. "I can prove what I say is true. The raider's ship probably has a copy of Queen Cassandra's announcement, because it was sent out to all the member worlds. You can see the young Draconian queen for yourself and hear her words."

"Why would any other world listen to a human queen who rules over warriors? In the entire universe, we alone are despised." The question came from one of the many elder warriors. She couldn't tell which had spoken.

"Where I come from, we have an intergalactic council of planets. Draconians were inducted a few years ago."

"They accepted us, even though our queens are ruthless?"

Looking over at the old man who spoke, she shook her head. "Hell no, your queens are all human, except the one little Draconian queen." Rubbing her temple, she searched her memory for more information on the alien queen. "Jesus, I cannot remember her name to save my life."

"This is something I would give much to see."

Nodding at the older warrior who looked like Larok, she understood why. "Anyways, you are the good guys where I'm from. Every trader has some fascinating tale about how Draconian warriors came to their rescue when they needed help. Your ships appear out of nowhere, fight off pirates and raiders and stuff like that, and then disappear into the black. Draconians even came up with some device that's cleaning the atmosphere on my dying home world to make it more habitable."

Larok's quiet voice interjected, "That must be why you seemed so thrilled to be found by me."

"Yes sir, that would be the reason. I don't have to worry too much about whether or not you're honorable. I already know you are, because the warriors prove it all the time in my sector of space. Sorry about the freak out earlier. I don't know what got into me."

The older man who resembled Larok spoke. "It heals a small ache in my soul to know that somewhere in the 'verse our brethren are respected."

"Are you and Larok related? You look a lot alike."

Preening a bit, the man replied, "Larok is my scion."

"The translation program is substituting the word son for scion."

"Forgive this foolish old warrior for failing to make introductions." Bowing his head slightly, he intoned. "My name is Jeron, scion of Drakon. Larok is indeed my son, to use your human term."

"My name is Hope, and I'm the scion of Andrew Burk. We're of Swiss descent, and my father died in the fall, so I don't know if I'm supposed to list that part in an official introduction. Anyways, it's real nice to meet you Mr. Jeron."

Regarding her warmly, he took a step closer. "It is nice to meet you as well, young queen. Congratulations on selecting my scion as your protector. He is well worthy of the honor." Turning to the other warriors, he delivered some distressing news. "Our aged Draconian queen has taken a turn for the worse. She can no longer lift her head or take sustenance. I fear she is little aware of the decisions we make regarding the operation of this ship."

Another whispered, "How we will function without a queen is anyone's guess. Our dream of freedom should be close at hand, but I worry how we will make that happen with no leadership in place."

Hope spoke up again. "I hate to keep butting my head into your personal affairs, and I'm real sorry to hear about your queen being sick, but I have something to say. You guys seem to be the oldest and wisest warriors on the ship. Why don't you just set up a ruling council? On Earth we vote our leaders into their positions." As she got lost talking about the ins and outs of the geopolitical systems on Earth, conversation swirled quietly around her."

One word sounded off around the room. "Agreed."

Finally getting excited, Hope offered, "Great, I'd be happy to help create some type of confidential voting process. Maybe warriors could all sign into a..."

Jeron stated solemnly. "You are well named, Queen Hope, for you give us hope of a better life. We select you to be our new queen."

Shock rippled through her body. After a stunned

moment, she said, "Yeah, well that's not as great an idea as it might seem. I know you warriors really put your women on a pedestal, and it's real cute that you call us all queens, but the cold hard fact is, we're just regular people. I don't know anything about politics or mother ships."

"We believe queens are born with an innate ability to lead, and their right to rule is irrefutable. Queens forged in a crucible of hardship and war, emerge stronger and more resilient."

Folding her arms over her chest, Hope dug in her heels. "We have a similar saying. What doesn't kill you only makes you stronger."

"Queens are born to rule."

"We're not; trust me on that one, okay?"

Jeron took a step closer as his gaze intensified. "If you were our queen, how would you recommend we proceed?"

Rubbing her arm, Hope perked up a little. "I'm fairly good at giving advice. Being an advisor seems like a good role for me." Thinking it over, she began to get motivated. "I guess the first thing I would do is put your dying queen in stasis. We don't want that parasite loose on the ship infecting anyone else when she passes. Maybe we could do some scans while she's in stasis and figure out how to remove the symbiont. Your queen's dying breath should be with dignity, not with a parasite controlling her mind."

"You are wise beyond your years, Queen Hope."

"I think we should also hunt down that raider ship, force them to give up the women they stole and suck all the information out of the databanks. Maybe we can find something in all that information to help us figure a way to key our wormhole generator to get us to the Naxis sector." Pausing to consider a new idea that had jumped into her brain, Hope plunged full steam ahead. "Or better yet, we confiscate their wormhole generator. I'll bet the squid dudes have all the information on how their own unit works in their computer banks. They would need that to train their operators, right?"

"I would assume so. You wish to return to your sector of space?"

"I want all of us to get the hell out of here. If you stay, some other queen will just scoop you up. I can't imagine that you would want that, when you can have freedom instead. You guys would love the new Draconian home world. It's lush, beautiful and loaded with rare gemstones and minerals. Everyone there is ridiculously happy from what I could make out from the news feeds on Earth."

"Your will be done, my queen."

"What? Wait, I never agreed to be your queen."

Ignoring her indignant tone, Jeron turned to his scion. "Take our new queen to rest in your quarters. I will make arrangements for a space to be created for her comfort."

When he bent to pick her up again, Larok's big muscular arms caught her notice. Shooting her hand out to stop him, Hope shoved his hands away. "I can walk. Your doctor says I'm fine."

"As you wish, my queen."

Sighing, she asked, "Can you just call me Hope?"

"Whatever demands you make will be my honor to obey, my imperious and miniature queen."

Glancing up at his face, she found his eyes held a hint of amusement. It looked good on him. "Are you trying to be funny? I can't quite tell with you."

Straightening back up, he replied, "I do not believe warriors are not permitted to have a sense of humor."

"Yea, I see it now. You definitely have a soldier's sense of humor."

His eyes shimmered with warmth, making her smile at their careless banter. Yeah, whatever this was flying back and forth between the two of them was going to be good. Hope could feel it all the way down to her bones.

LAROK

WALKING WITH ONE ARM WRAPPED SNUGLY AROUND his new queen's waist, Larok made his way from the loading bay to his quarters. The corridors were lined with silent warriors, their backs pressed respectfully against the wall. Each male was eager to get a glimpse of their new human queen. Not only was she beautiful, with her flame-colored strands, she had chosen a simple warrior for her protector over highly respected breeders. Larok could easily understand why they were fascinated enough to come out in droves.

Queen Hope seemed as curious about the warriors as they were about her. Though she didn't speak to them or slow her pace, she was alert and looked briefly at each warrior they passed. As soon as the door to his quarters closed, his bunkmates stepped back against the wall to stand guard in the traditional manner.

Looking nervously around, Queen Hope appeared to grow uncomfortable. "Gosh, I don't mean to be an imposition."

Guiding her towards the cleansing unit, he replied

sincerely. "No queen could be an imposition, least of all a small human queen like yourself."

Rolling her eyes, she replied dryly. "I guess fighting off an alien ship full of creepy squid men and having to rescue me is just all in day's work for you."

"Perhaps not, but I am pleased to have the opportunity to serve. My brethren will make you a nest to rest upon and obtain food while we cleanse."

"I don't know what a nest is, but I'm really tired, so I'd probably sleep anywhere that didn't involve twigs and thorns. Don't worry about food. I'd be happy with another food bar like we had on the shuttle. I'm not picky."

Several of his bunkmates chirped their disapproval of her being fed a food ration. Larok wasn't looking forward to the hearing them speak their mind on that subject. As soon as the door to the cleansing room shut, his queen began to walk around inspecting the small room. The misting heads protruded about waist high from the wall at measured intervals around the room. He realized rather quickly that since his queen was much shorter than a warrior he would have to lift her up to use them or the mist would shoot into her face, perhaps choking her.

"Is there any chance you could show me to a toilet? I really have to go." For some reason her face turned a lovely shade of pink when she asked. Even through the smudges of dirt, she looked adorable.

Walking swiftly to her, he hit a bar above the mister and a unit flipped out of the wall with an oval opening in the front. "If you will remove your clothing, I will lift you onto the unit."

"Never mind, I'm fine."

"If you do not remove impurities from your body, you will become ill."

Rolling her eyes again, she responded, "I know that. I'm human, not stupid."

"Then what is the problem?"

"Well for starters, I don't pee out of my stomach. Why are these things so weird?"

Opening his pants, he walked up to the unit and pressed his lower abdomen to the unit, careful to ensure a tight seal between the unit and his body."

Her hands flew to her face. "I can't believe you just did that!"

Leaning on the wall with one hand, his head swiveled around to look at her. "You have my sincere apologies, Queen Hope. I was under the impression you needed a visual demonstration."

By this point her face was the color of the strands coming out of her head. "Why is everything here so freaking difficult?" Sucking in a breath, she explained. "Human women sit to relieve themselves, we don't just belly up to . . . whatever this is."

"I should have realized that. Our queens are built the same way." Pulling himself away, he refastened his pants and jerked another unit from the wall, revealing a saddle shaped basin. Twisting it around one quarter of the way, he gestured to it. "If you will allow, I can lift you onto the basin. This is the sink a small number of my brethren use to tend to their molting. It is the best option I have to offer."

"Fine, but don't look."

Unsure what she was referring to, he squeezed his eyes shut. Within moments her hands covered his, and she spoke. "Lift me now."

He did as she asked, and she maneuvered herself onto the basin. "Let go, and turn around please." Again his compliance was immediate.

"You know something? I'm beginning to wish for that stupid bucket the raiders gave us. At least I didn't need anyone to help me use the darn thing. I honestly don't want to be a nuisance, but we have got to work out something more practical than this."

"Again, I apologize. Caretakers are usually tasked with caring for queens, not sentinels."

"It's not your fault that nothing on a Draconian ship is human sized. I didn't mean to imply that it was."

Bits of her dirty clothing landed on the floor beside him. "What do I push to get the shower going? Don't turn around, just tell me."

"If you are still sitting on the basin, push the bar protruding from antar...I mean the left."

He heard the mister come on. "Is all well my queen?"

"Yes, is this pump for soap?"

"If soap is cleanser, then yes it is."

"In that case, I'm better than well. This is amazing. I can't stand being dirty."

"Me either, my queen." Stepping forward, he was careful to keep his back to her as he pulled off his clothing and used the mister on the other side of the room.

"Wow, you warriors don't care who sees your bare backside."

Feeling something loosen in his chest at the happy tone of her voice, he replied without looking. "We do not. No warrior cares enough to look at another warrior's body. We are nude around each other often."

"Cut it out, Larok. You're making me think naughty thoughts about naked warriors."

Knowing that she was teasing him, he replied brazenly with playful banter of his own. "Will you turn pink again if we leave the cleansing room without clothing?"

There was a moment of silence before she answered. "I can put back on my clothing."

Hitting the button to turn off his mister, Larok tried not to laugh as shook out his wings. Marching out the door, he went in search of clean clothing.

The moment the door slid closed behind him, the other warriors began speaking.

"You cannot leave your queen unattended."

"How did you earn the strange alien queen's trust so quickly?"

"Why would you give her a food bar? That is no fit food for a queen."

Staring at his brethren, he almost chortled at their chiding advice.

"I found her clothing. It is not fit for a queen, but it is clean. I pulled you out some under things as well."

Bowing his head slightly at his brother, Larok intoned, "Thank you for the clothing, Calen. My queen does not enjoy being naked in front of other warriors." Turning to the other warriors, he explained. "Queen Hope was abducted and starved on the enemy vessel. I gave her the only food I had, and she not only thanked me, she broke off pieces and fed them to me."

Astonished noises came from his bunkmates.

"I must return to her. Please excuse me, my brothers."

Turning on his heel, he reentered the cleansing room to find his pale queen trying to dismount from the basin without him. Her tiny pale backside immediately caught his notice. May the goddess forgive him, he tried not to look at her queenly treasures, but he could hardly help himself, since her struggle bared everything a warrior would wish to see. Rushing to her side, he barely got there in time to catch her from falling. "You should wait for assistance, my queen. What if you had fallen?"

Giving him a shove back, she flipped her wet hair out of her face and scowled up at him. "I probably would have ended up with a bruise. At the worst. It was only a three- or four-foot drop. Larok, you have got to lighten up if you're going to be my protector."

Pushing the bar just above her head, he stared down into her upturned face as the jets blew out warm air to dry their bodies. His queen immediately lifted her hands and began running her fingers through her long red strands.

"I am pleased that your red spots did not wash off. They are quite lovely." It was a brash thing to say, but he had been chosen by her. Therefore, it stood to reason that he would be expected to produce complimentary verbalizations. In any case it was true. The red speckles on her face were captivating.

Laughing, she responded playfully. "They're called freckles, and I would erase every single one if I could."

Dropping his eyes to her voluptuous chest, he searched for more of the freckles. "Do they decorate your entire body or only the top part?"

Baring her blunt teeth in the traditional mating gesture, she chided him, "Turn around, you big flirt."

Quickly complying with her request, he held out the long under top his brother had found. "This is all we have for you to wear at the moment. I am certain clothing is being fabricated for you even as we speak."

Snatching it from his outstretched hand, she responded, "Again, I'm not choosey. As long as it's clean and covers my body, I'm happy."

"You are easy to please, for a queen."

"On Earth I didn't own anything but the clothes on my

back, and they were nothing to be proud of. It makes a person humble."

Quickly pulling on the under bottoms to cover his lower half, he turned around to find her running her fingers through her hair again. Stepping forward, he assisted her in ensuring there were no knots in her filaments.

"You're one helpful warrior. Are we really going to get some sleep? I'm exhausted."

Wrapping a wing around her, he guided her back out to the main room. "You have been through a harrowing ordeal, Queen Hope. You will eat and drink your fill then we will regenerate."

"It's real cute that you call sleeping regenerating. I suppose it is in a way." Coming to a stop, she remarked, "Wow, what is all this?"

His fellow warriors had pushed two sleeping platforms together and stacked all the rest of the hovering platforms against one wall. Their nest had been layered with fresh bedding. Though the nest was the first item to catch his eye, he suspected that his queen was referring to the small table that was laden with food.

"Come, I will assist you in selecting food."

"Do you have doma bread? I ended up tasting a piece while I was on earth. They started importing the doma plant because it's so healthy and prolific."

"It is thought of as a nuisance plant on our home world. Doma is considered a coarse food, worthy only of nourishing warriors."

"I don't care what anyone says, I think it tastes fantastic. It's all the rage on my dying home world."

Larok caught his sibling's eye, and Calen scurried away to retrieve some from their storage unit. Sitting his queen down in a chair, he looked over the selections. With a pair of pinchers, he carefully created a platter of bite-sized pieces, in order for her to sample their offerings.

"Wow, that's a lot of food. We should invite everyone over to eat."

"Warriors dine on whatever is left over. That is the natural order of things between warriors and queens."

She glanced up at him with wide eyes. "It'll all get cold by then."

"You are considerate to worry over us. I promise there is no need."

Not heeding his words at all, she jumped from her seat and began to call the other warriors. "Food is for sharing. Come and eat with me." The surprised males slowly moved forward as she asked.

"Everything looks so delicious. What's your favorite food, Larok?"

Pointing to small bit of vegetable rolled in a dried leaf, he said, "I like the avada. It is mild tasting. I believe you will like it, Queen Hope."

"I'm sure I will. Let's try some together. I don't know what these eating utensils are, but they're very much like chopsticks on Earth, only hinged together on one end."

"We call them pinchers."

"I can see why." Taking the pincher, she pulled out a bite of avada from the box he'd made for her. "Open up, handsome."

"I don't think it's appropriate for a queen to feed a warrior."

"Quick now, I'm going to drop it."

He opened his mouth and waited, hiding his inner trembling, until she gently laid the tiny bite of food in his mouth. Larok watched her gracefully turn back to the table and closed his eyes. She picked up another piece for herself and ate it standing up. "Oh my goodness, that's so good." Looking around at the other warriors, who weren't eating but only sitting and awkwardly watching, she said, "Here, everyone has to try a bite."

Most of the warriors had pulled up seats or boxes to sit on, and the rest had dropped down on the floor. The little queen walked around, dropping a vegetable roll in every warrior's hand. For someone who stated she was exhausted, their small ruler seemed rather energetic. Larok saw she was trying hard to make sure no one was left out or had cause to be angry with her.

His sibling, Calen, arrived with their box of doma, and Larok motioned for him to give it to their queen. She was pleased by the simple gift. The day before, Larok would have been upset that his entire stash of doma had been given to the warriors, but he couldn't find it in his heart to disapprove of his queen's generous nature.

Finally, she sank down in her chair and looked around at the assembled warriors. "Umm, you're all pretty quiet."

Larok held out his hand to escort her to her to the sleeping platform. "We are not used to having a queen mixing so freely among warriors, much less one in our quarters."

"Sorry about that. Everyone's been a really good sport about me horning in on their space. I wish there was something I could do to repay your kindness, but I'm not sure how helpful I could be on a spaceship. On Earth, I just did odd jobs. I learn pretty fast, though. If someone wanted to teach me a job, I promise to pay close attention and do my best."

Skipping over the fact that she was their queen, and that came with a large assortment of responsibilities, Larok responded diplomatically. "Warriors tend to err on the side of caution where queens are concerned. I am sorry if we seem quiet. We are not used to queens speaking so freely with us."

"It's probably me. I tend to talk a lot, so everyone else seems quiet by comparison."

"Though we aren't used to a conversational queen, I find your manner delightful."

"You should try to get used to outgoing women. There will be a hundred other jaws flapping when we rescue my friends. Once they come aboard, no warrior will be able to get a word in edgewise. I'm sure they'll be interested in learning about Draconian culture."

"That is nice of you to say, but I believe the other warriors are scheduled to attend to their duties for the next few hours so you can rest." The warriors took that as their cue to give their new queen some time to herself. "I will stand watch."

"I don't need anyone to stand guard over me. At least I don't think I do."

"Queens are ever and always guarded aboard our ships. It is due more to tradition than because of real danger."

"That sounds silly to me. Why don't you try to get some sleep as well? I don't think I'd be able to sleep with someone staring at me."

Everything about this human queen was foreign to Larok. Normally, queens would issue commands and ultimatums. Delay or refusal was not an option. Queen Hope seemed to be negotiating for what she wished. It was a strange approach to dealing with a warrior, and kept him off balance. "I must admit to never have given much thought to what has always been, my queen. Our old queen had a dozen warriors standing guard while she slept. Even I have to admit such a number was unnecessary, my queen."

"Please call me Hope." She climbed onto the platform, made herself comfortable, and pulled up the covering. "How about we take turns guarding for each other?"

Her innocent question took him by surprise. "It is my honor to stand guard over you. It is what warriors were made for."

She pulled back the covering and looked up at him. The red strands fell across her brow, and she did not move them away. "Where I come from, good-looking guys are for cuddling up to. Come sleep beside me."

The thought of being with her had Larok moving before he even stopped to consider all the consequences of sharing a sleeping space with a queen.

Queen Hope smiled at him again, murmuring sleepily. "We both sleep, or neither of us sleeps."

"As you wish, my queen."

She pulled the coarse covering up over them, turned her back to him, and scooted over until she was touching his body. Clearly, cuddling was sharing body heat. It was clever of his queen to utilize a male for warmth.

Yawning, she looked over her shoulder. "See? Isn't that better than standing?"

"If it pleases you, my queen."

"Yeah, yeah, yeah. You getting some shut-eye pleases the hell out of me, handsome."

Larok watched her get comfortable, and then she went still. She'd called him attractive. The reality of being chosen was slowly sinking in. He was sharing a queen's sleeping platform. That was about as chosen as a warrior could be. She would eventually choose other warriors as protectors, so he would have to make the most of having her undivided attention while it lasted.

It was true that when the goddess smiled, anything was

possible, even a simple warrior being a selected as a queen's protector. Concern creased his brow. He normally would have visited his youngling, but having a queen kept him from gazing upon the growing shell surrounding his unborn child.

The wires of flame growing from her head were so long that some were near his face. He wrapped a few around his finger, only to discover that they were soft and pliable, especially now that she had cleaned the dirt away. He caressed his face with the strands and breathed the essence of his queen. Sweetness of flowers. Salt. The smell of dreams.

Larok couldn't help but wonder what his new queen would make of him having a little one. He worried that she would cast him aside for already being bred, or that she would wish his unborn child to be disposed of. His chest ached at the thought of losing his only child. It would be better that she never knew of the tiny warrior's existence, he decided. The thought of lying to her twice made him feel like utaka larva. Still, what choice did he have?

The little queen tossed and turned in her sleep. The second she reached out for him, Larok moved closer, wrapping his arm around her and pulling up one wing to cover their entwined bodies. She snuggled closer, draping one leg over his body. He couldn't be sure, but it seemed like she was still sleeping. Having her warm soft body against him was confusing, thrilling, and aroused his breeding lust.

He forced himself to calm down and closed his eyes. It went without saying that his two siblings were standing guard outside the door. He could rest easy, with his new queen sharing his body heat. Larok tumbled off to sleep with a new kind of hope growing in his chest. Maybe everything would turn out fine.

The next thing he knew, his sire was shaking him gently

awake. He carefully disengaged from his queen and slipped out of the room with his father.

"Is all well, my sire?"

"Your new queen *commanded* you to lie with her?"

"You have raised me to know the difference between right and wrong, sire. I would never force myself on a queen. She insisted on a human custom called cuddling."

"The translation program is substituting the word embrace."

"It seems to be 'embracing for a long period of time in order to secure warmth from a male.' I do not fully understand it myself."

"You seem to be proficient at this human custom. Pleasing your queen is all that matters."

"I do not think human queens can be displeased. Not in the ways we are used to seeing with our own queens. No matter what happens, Queen Hope simply adjusts and all is well."

"If what you say is true, it will make caring for a multitude of human queens easier. We must be careful in our endeavors, for I have no wish to lose even one if it can be helped."

"Have you secured our elder queen?"

"Abraka is safely secured in a stasis unit. We filled the room with a gas that put her to sleep. After that it was easy to place her in stasis."

"That was clever."

"We had no wish to take her against her will. In her condition, she might have been injured."

"No one would want that, my sire."

"Our new queen has commanded us to track down the ship filled with her human companions. That should certainly be our next mission."

Larok looked anxiously at the door behind him. Even with his two younger brothers guarding his new queen, it felt strange to leave her alone. His sire's hand landed on his shoulder. "Think not on your queen. Your brethren will see to her safety."

Calen could be trusted to care properly for a queen. However, his younger brother was far from responsible. Still, his queen's commands must be obeyed, so he followed his father.

WAKING UP TOOK MORE EFFORT THAN USUAL. Realizing she was on a soft mattress with warm bedding, Hope bolted up. Something wasn't right. She hadn't slept like this since before the fall. Memories came crashing through her mind of being on the Taladar ship, getting abducted and then rescued by the hot Draconian guy.

Rubbing her eyes didn't help. Everything was still blurry. Falling back down onto her back, Hope struggled to get her head together. Her eyes were puffy from sleeping too much, it was that and nothing more, she told herself sternly.

She reached for the opposite side of the nest, expecting to find Larok there. When her hand landed on nothing but cold bedding, confusion was like a bucket of ice water on the dream she'd been having of him. She forced herself up again and swung her legs over the side of the bed. Taking in her surroundings for the first time, she saw they had moved her to an entirely new room. Doing a double take between her hovering bed and the door, she estimated the door frame wasn't large enough to accommodate the bed. Then she remembered they had created it from two slim warrior-sized hovering sleeping cots.

Why in the hell wouldn't they just wake her up? Scrubbing her hands over her face, she swallowed back a frustrated groan. This was just the kind of thing that wouldn't happen if Paws was still alive. He would have sounded off, waking her up to face the day like a real live person. Instead she got left behind because they had clearly mistaken her for some kind of frail, weak female.

Then again, she couldn't really blame them for arriving at the wrong conclusion. She had been acting all kinds of weird since arriving on their vessel. Her emotions had been all over the place. One minute she told her handsome protector not to touch her or even look at her, but last night she vaguely remembered snuggling right up to him when she was in a sleep-induced fog. How comically inconsistent could a person be?

None of that mattered. All the swinging back and forth like a well-oiled pendulum was coming to a stop right now. She needed to locate real clothing and find something useful to do with her time. The first thing that came to mind was helping find her friends.

A deep masculine voice she didn't recognize floated across the room. "I see you are awake, Queen Hope. Welcome to the *Obsidian*."

Her head came up fast, searching the room for the man speaking to her. Her eyes found a bare-chested warrior wearing long flowing pants. He seemed to be organizing the room or something. "Who are you?"

"I am Tamen. I served the last queen and will be happy to be your caretaker as well."

"I'm not old, therefore I don't need a caretaker. Besides

I already have a hot guy looking out for me. Speaking of which, where is my Larok?"

Smiling faintly, he moved closer. "He is attending to your business. You do need a personal body assistant, my queen. Who will bathe you, dress you and polish your claws?"

Smothering a smile, she tried to stay serious. "Humans do that sort of thing for themselves."

"I heard all about the debacle when you last attempted to care for yourself. I've already scolded your protector for allowing you to almost fall."

A laugh bubbled up and out of her mouth before she could stop herself. It was thinking about poor Larok getting scolded by this man who was half his size that tickled her funny bone. "Leave the poor man alone. Larok only did what I asked him to do. Falling isn't the end of the world. I've fallen a bunch of times, and you know what? I just get up, dust myself off, and get my sweet ass moving again."

"You look small and fragile. I should think that falling might break you."

"Humans are really hardy and resilient. After spending a little time around us, you'll be amazed."

"Would you like me to draw you a bath?"

"Like you said, I just had a shower before I went to sleep. Look, would it be at all possible to have some clothing?"

"I have fabricated you several gowns to choose from."

Hope's mouth fell open. "Why in the heck would I want to wear a gown on a spaceship? That makes absolutely no sense."

Frowning, Tamen appeared confused. "A gown is a mark of status."

"Hells bells, I don't care about status. Can you make uniforms in my size?"

Tamen leaned closer, clearly confused. "What kind of uniform, my queen?"

"I want a uniform like the warriors wear. It needs to be something that allows me to run, climb, and fight."

"Why in the 'verse would you want to do that?"

"I need to be able to move if I'm going to help get my friends back."

"I believe your protector is seeing to that even now."

Jumping out of the bed, Hope smiled up at the half-naked caretaker. "Larok's the best. I really like him." When the man didn't respond, she palm-smacked her forehead. "Well, of course you're nice as well. I didn't mean to imply that you weren't or anything."

Though he didn't quite smile, Tamen's eyes sparkled with mirth. "What they say is true. You are much different from the queens we have known."

Never missing a chance to drive her point home, she replied, "Yet, I'm certain they wore uniforms."

"Our queens wear uniforms only for battle, my queen. Since you insist, I might be able to secure a young warrior's uniform for you."

Barely able to contain her excitement, Hope gushed. "Thank you so much. I appreciate it more than you know."

Raising a tiny communications device to his lips, Tamen spoke into it. Hope wandered around the huge room, wearing only the knee length sleeping shirt Larok had found for her the night before. The room was luxurious beyond anything she'd seen, with several seating areas, what appeared to be a lap pool, and a shelf filled with items whose purpose she couldn't even begin to understand. The well-appointed furnishing seemed designed for comfort rather than utility. She guessed the warriors made this space for the hundred human women they were rescuing. The accommodations surpassed anything she'd ever heard of on a spaceship, or on a planet, for that matter.

Worry twisted in her gut over the women that she'd left behind. The raiders were careless in the treatment of their human cargo, often forgetting to feed them and change out the buckets they relieved themselves in. No one had bathed since being brought onto the raider ship. Their situation was precarious. A million things could go wrong that could result in sickness and even death.

The doors opened and four warriors entered. Two were wearing the same billowing pants Tamen wore; only they were carrying one of the trademark gunmetal gray uniforms, same as the other crew members wore. The other two appeared to be related to Larok. They had his exact shade of coloring, wings and similar overly muscular builds. One she recognized as the guy who brought doma the evening before. Getting sidetracked, she gushed. "You even found me some boots! You guys are amazing. This is just what I need."

The day was looking up, assuming it was day instead of night. It was hard to tell on a spaceship. Rushing over to the newcomers, she waited to be given her clothing. Tamen gathered the items and turned to her. "We typically wear the uniform over our undergarments for comfort's sake."

Smoothing her hand down the garment she thought was a nightshirt, she responded happily. "I love this fabric. It's thin, soft and really comfortable. Did they tell you that we're going to be having a hundred women like me on board this ship very soon?"

"Ten times ten queens? I didn't know there would so many. Will they require uniforms as well?"

"They'll need to use the cleansing room and trust me, most won't care what they wear, as long as it's clean. I know providing basic necessities for such a large group will a terrible inconvenience, but they are in a bad way aboard the raider. Anything we could do to make them feel comfortable would be nice."

Looking all kinds of serious, Tamen asked, "What do you suggest, my queen?"

"When we get them into the loading bay, it would be nice if we had hydration packets and food bars available. I hadn't eaten in three days prior to being rescued. We were all pretty dehydrated. Maybe we could get our healer in there to do health scans. After that, just getting them clean and letting them rest will be a godsend."

"Do they have young?"

"Nope. There is a small grouping of girls who aren't quite old enough to mate. We should probably keep them together."

"Forgive me for bringing up a delicate subject. Will the all the queens require breeders? If so, we have a handful of warriors experienced in tending the needs of a queen on board."

Trying her best not to laugh, Hope took a moment to formulate an intelligent answer to his absurd question. "Human Queens normally select their protector from the males they happen to meet. On your new home world Queen Cassandra asked the warriors to separate into pairs. Some of the women were really excited about the Taladar because they have family units of three men for each woman. I suspect that the majority of women would be happy with two warriors in a family unit, since that's what they were expecting anyway. Some might prefer one-on-one pair bonding."

The warriors made a small trilling sound she was coming to associate with shock under their breath. It was something she was growing to expect when they were confronted with the unexpected. Tamen swallowed thickly. "We noticed you chose a simple warrior for your first protector. Will the women be looking to link with our breeders in particular?"

"Most of them don't know a thing about Draconian mating customs. When they look at warriors, they don't see class or a hierarchy. They just see hot men who might be open to having a relationship with them. We also have a few older women who are looking for age mates, so if some of the elder warriors teamed up to approach them individually, I'm certain at least some of them would appreciate the opportunity to have age mates."

"Thank you for the wealth of information on human mating. We will begin work on providing for ten times ten queens. I will take special care to ensure everything is as it should be, my queen."

Leaning over, she gave Tamen a hug. "Thanks for everything you're doing. You are all so awesome that I don't even have words to say."

It didn't take long to get dressed and pull her hair back into a top knot. Tamen slowed her down long enough to add a strange silver utility belt with a dagger and the smallest laser pistol she'd ever seen. Wheedling and charming her guards into taking her to see Larok took almost no effort at all.

HOPE

WALKING THROUGH THE SHIP WITH TWO WARRIORS AT her back was weird but comforting. She sure was getting used to being spoiled rotten by the nice warriors! Wouldn't it be terrible if the Taladarians forced them to fulfil their contracts?

When the door to the bridge glided open, she saw Larok at a navigation station. Sliding into the chair next to him, she murmured. "I wondered where you'd run off to."

"Why would you wonder such a thing?"

Trailing one finger around the seam of his uniform at the shoulder, she responded shyly. "I missed you when I woke up."

His horns perked up, he started to breathe faster, and his facial expression couldn't hide his excitement. "You jest with me?"

"Nope. I thought you might have gotten bored with me already."

"Never. I am about your business, just as you commanded."

Yawning, she murmured, "It was more of a request than a command, with a little begging on the side." Realizing what he was talking about, Hope thought of her friends on the raiders' ship, and excitement strummed through her body. "Have we found any trace of the raider?"

"Are you sure you wish to be involved in this situation? You can rest easy in the queen's chamber while we track the vessel and retrieve the queens."

Looking at him intently, she smiled. "No way, hot stuff. I go where you go. I'm ready to help bring that ship to heel—any way I can."

"You wish revenge on the ones who tormented you. This is something I understand all too well. Allow your protector to act in your stead."

"I want, no I *need* to help." Resting her hand on the tiny weapon at her side she spoke earnestly. "They gave me a weapon and everything. I'll use it if I have to."

"The tiny weapon on your hip is one of most powerful in our arsenal. Do not draw unless you are in great danger."

"Thanks for the heads up."

After a slightly pause, he explained, "Boarding the enemy ship will be dangerous. I do not wish to risk you, my Hope. It would wound my soul if you were injured."

"That's real sweet. The thing is, I can calm the women down and get them moving. If you boys go in all by yourselves, they might panic, thinking they are just getting taken for mating by yet another alien race."

His horns froze in place and he turned to look at her. "Many warriors aboard this vessel are looking forward to wooing their own human queen. Therefore, we are taking them with the hope of mating."

Smiling at him, she responded playfully. "That's our

little secret. They'll probably just assume that's true since I took you to mate. If not, we won't let the cat out of the bag."

"I do not understand human speech, even though my translation program spits out the words."

Changing the subject, she asked, "How close are we to their ship?"

"We followed their exhaust trail, and though it is somewhat degraded, we believe they are in orbit around a small planet. We are nearing the area now."

Dropping his hands from the console, he looked at her. His expression was more serious than usual. Hope sat up straight and prepared for bad news.

"My father was Queen Abraka's first. Therefore, he will be your first as well." It was a statement, not a question. Chewing her bottom lip, Hope tried to figure out why he was telling her what they all already understand to be a fact.

The older man's voice sounded off from a console nearby. "That is, unless you have someone else in mind to command your military, Queen Hope."

Glancing over her shoulder at Jeron, she tried to keep the frustration out of her voice. "I have no idea what you're talking about, and I never agreed to be your queen."

"You were chosen by the elders aboard this vessel. The decision of who will be first is your decision."

Sighing, she gave up trying to argue with him. "Now is not the time to upset the apple cart. It would probably be best to continue letting the guy's who's been doing an excellent job to, uh, operate in his current capacity."

Frowning, the older warrior clearly didn't understand the apple cart expression. However, he was able to get the gist of what she was saying. He dipped his head respectfully. "Yes, my queen."

Rubbing the vein throbbing in her temple, Hope realized she hadn't eaten or drunk anything since waking. "Is there a fountain nearby? I need to drink."

Larok reached under the console and then handed her a small hydration pouch, similar to the one they drank from on his shuttle. Popping it open, she pulled out the short, straw-like drinking port. After taking a refreshing sip, Hope held it out for the busy navigator to sip. Without complaint, he took a long draw. "Thank you, my queen."

"You're welcome, handsome."

His lips quirked up at the corners, but he didn't stop what he was doing at the control panel. A Klaxon sounded. Jeron announced, "We have picked them up on our sensors. I am scanning the ship for the queens now." Breathless moments passed before the elder warrior spoke again. "I am showing a total of ten-times-twelve queens plus seven."

"Wow, a hundred and twenty-seven women? That's more than I counted when I was in the holding bay."

Jeron chirped in frustration. "They are keeping ten times three queens in a secondary loading bay. For what purpose, I do not know."

Hope stood up and walked over to Jeron's screen. "I've got a really bad feeling about the women in the other bay."

"As do I. I am getting a ghost of another signal. I can't get a read on whether it's an injured queen or some kind of energy sucker."

Guessing, she asked, "Beings who feed on a person's energy?"

Nodding, he continued trying to focus in on the last life-sign. "They are rare, but not unheard-of in this sector of space."

Hope thought it over and decided it was mostly likely a

sick woman. "Can we call every healer we have out for this one? I'd like Kalar to join the boarding party."

"Yes, Queen Hope. That is an outstanding idea." Jeron immediately sent a message to the medical unit.

Pacing back and forth between stations, Hope tried to stay out of their way. She couldn't help but wonder why some of the women were being kept separate from the others. She prayed they hadn't been used as playthings by the horrible squid men. The twisted creatures seemed to think that burning human skin with their suckers was amusing. Maybe they didn't realize how painful it was. Either that or they simply didn't care.

"I want to speak to them."

"Inadvisable, my queen. If they realize we have discovered their location, they will surely know you have come to secure the release of your human companions. It is reasonable to suspect they may vent the imprisoned queens in an effort to get us to stop pursuing them."

Rubbing her hands over her face, Hope forced herself to sit down again. "We don't want them doing anything stupid. I guess we need to sneak up on them and try to board before they realize what we're doing."

Another warrior spoke up. "Their vessel is primitive, compared to ours. It has also been damaged. I do not believe they have the capacity to scan for us."

Larok said, "We could take ten shuttles loaded with warriors and simply overwhelm their defenses."

Jeron nodded. "Our reflective armor will keep them from seeing us until it's too late."

Hope quickly pointed out, "Those aliens are shifty devils. I worry that they will use the women to keep us away from them."

"There is a docking ring very close to the loading bay. If

we have a team of seasoned warriors enter at that point, it will put us within striking distance of those guarding your friends. The ones in the secondary bay are isolated and more difficult to access. We'll have to fight our way through the ship to get to them."

"I don't like risking the warriors. Isn't there some way of temporary disabling the squid to avoid the hand-to-hand combat?"

Kalar stepped on the bridge. "If we could access their database, I might be able to fabricate an airborne intoxicant keyed to their unique biology that will render them unable to fight. I would hesitate to do that before getting a look at their physiology."

"If they are anything like the squids of Earth, practically nothing can hurt them. When our oceans became so polluted that other fish began going extinct, the squids just absorbed every kind of contaminant they came into contact with. Even though their bodies tested positive for high concentrations of what we considered poisonous substances, they still survived until the sea became too acidic to support life."

Kalar seemed intrigued. "You are a wealth of informa-tion, Queen Hope."

Turing pink, she acknowledged, "I was kind of a book-worm growing up."

Larok interrupted, "I advise that we simply attack the creatures and take the queens from them. Studying them will take precious time the queens do not have. We have no idea what has happened to them since my Hope left that ship. The aliens holding the captives may have escalated their abuse. We need to get them out now."

Folding her arms over her chest, she glared at him.

"We're going to get some warriors killed if we're not real careful."

"Better warriors than queens. We are made for fighting. Your queen friends need our protection."

Jeron stood. "My scion is correct. The queens are our priority, not the warriors."

Hope could see which way the wind was blowing on this one. The thing was, they were right. "Let's cull only the best warriors and make sure they are armored and heavily armed. If we're going for a full frontal assault, I want to give them best chance at survival we possibly can under the circumstances."

Jeron nodded. "I agree. I will assign a team to locate and remove the wormhole generator, assuming it can be removed without destroying it."

"Draconians are technologically advanced. I believe our techs can figure it out." Looking from Larok to Jaron, Hope waited for one of them to weigh in.

The older man's lips pressed into a thin line. "I pray that you are right, my queen. Once the warriors are aboard and have secured the queens, we need to make getting them to safety the number one priority. When we are safely away, we will fire on their weapons array, lest they simply target the shuttles with their laser cannons. Slipping in, we will go unnoticed because they are not expecting an attack from the *Obsidian*. Once the battle begins, they will be keeping a close eye out for anything that moves, especially escaping shuttles."

"We're really doing this thing, aren't we?"

Larok nodded, "Yes, my Hope. We will save as many of your friend queens as possible this day. We should prepare for battle. Our seasoned warriors will exit the shuttle first. You will stay behind me at all times. When we breach the bay with the queens, you will speak to them and soothe their worries."

She stepped close to Larok and put her arms high up around his neck. Into that intimate space she said, "Thank you for saving me and for helping rescue the others. I won't be trouble, I promise." He looked worried about her accompanying them on such a dangerous mission. Truth be told, the last thing in the 'verse Hope wanted was to end up back on that ship again. If she hadn't thought she had something to add to the mission, she would have gladly stayed behind.

Larok's hand came up, tilting her face to look at him. The expression on his normally expressionless warrior's face nearly took her breath away. His dark eyes held a mixture of adoration tinged with a hint of lust. "Thank you for worrying about our warriors being in danger. Not many queens care about such things."

The poor man must have been treated poorly by their symbiont-infested queens to be grateful for something like that. His hands dropped to her waist, and he pulled her closer. Being in his arms felt more right than anything she'd ever experienced before. Cupping his face in her hands, she allowed herself to soak in the joy of the moment. "Most human women would feel the same about putting males in harm's way. I'm nothing special in that regard."

"To me, you are unique in all the ways that matter." He leaned down and rubbed his face up one side and down the other side of her face.

"Is that a Draconian display of affection?"

Nodding, his dark eyes seemed to gaze into her very soul. He could be intense at times. Maybe it was having to deal with a woman when he'd thought such a responsibility would never fall upon his shoulders. It was affecting him.

Even as the other warriors moved around them, making

final preparations for their mission, Hope couldn't tear herself away from her favorite warrior. "Do you think that once this is all over, and we make it back to normal space, there might be a chance that you and I could make a go of it together?"

"We are together already, my Hope. I offered all that I am to you, and you accepted me. I have enjoyed your undivided attention and provided cuddles according to your human customs. It would grieve me deeply if you cast me away once we reach our new home world."

"In that case, let me introduce you to my favorite display of human affection." Reaching way up, she cupped her hand behind his neck and pulled him down for a kiss. The moment before their lips touched was wrought with tension. They were breathing the same air, and he smelled like hot, sexy male. Lifting onto her toes, she ghosted her lips across his. At first he was slightly hesitant. Seconds flew by, and she began to pull back.

Having none of that, her eager warrior lifted her into his arms, wrapped his wings about her, and picked up where she left off. Her feet dangling from the floor felt awkward, so Hope wrapped her arms around his neck and her legs around his waist. She felt the provocative pose would go unnoticed since his wings shielded most of her body from curious eyes. The sound of angry chirping warriors slowly faded away, as they shared their very first kiss. How long they kissed, she couldn't say, but when they finally came up for air, the room was totally empty.

"I hope they didn't leave without us."

"Fear not my precious queen." Larok's eyes slid away. "I believe my mating scent drove them away."

Cupping his face in her hands, she murmured. "That can't be true. You smell fabulous."

"To queens perhaps my scent is appealing. It is an evolutionary advantage meant to lure a queen and drive away all the males competing for her attention."

Tracing the length of his jawline, she purred. "It's working like a charm."

"I love how you speak to me, as though I am your equal."

Laughing, she responded playfully. "We're not equals, babe. I'd have to get up pretty early in the morning to compete on an equal footing with a hot warrior like you."

For the very first time, his expression lit up with a full smile. It made him twice as gorgeous as he was before. "Come, my Hope. Let us ready ourselves for battle. I'm eager to retrieve your friend queens so we might rest again together this night."

"I hope you're thinking really dirty thoughts because I sure am."

"It is best that I do not speak of such. I'm barely hanging onto my clear thinking as it is." He slid her down his front until her feet touched the floor. "We should go. It is not appropriate to have the flight crew manning their positions from secondary back up stations. They need the bridge to be most effective." His voice was tight like he was forcing himself to get moving. Taking her by the hand, he led her out into the corridor. Only his two brothers remained. Each of them covered their nose at the same time.

"Your smell is strong and perfectly revolting, Larok."

"If I were a true breeder, the entire ship would be forced to suffer my mating scent."

"Since you're not, only we suffer."

Hope had to laugh at their pithy conversation. "Whoever said warriors aren't funny?"

Larok's head turned to look at her, his horns coming up

in what she was beginning to think of as an angry display. "Warriors are not normally credited with having much of a personality, much less traits like humor." Thumping his muscular chest with one fist, he stared down at her. "The queens have used our similarity to justify making us expendable."

His brother spoke quietly. "It is true, what my sibling has said. We are seen as being so similar that one can hardly distinguish one from the other of us."

Trying not to seem smug, Hope quipped, "Shows how much your queens know. I not only see all your individual differences, I even managed to pick out my handsome soon-to-be-husband's relatives just by sight."

"You are clever, and pretty, and very conversational, Queen Hope." Calen's very nice compliment made her feel embarrassed. Reaching out to Calen, she ran her hands over his uniform. "Are you hiding doma in your pockets? I think I can smell it on you."

Sighing, he slipped a hand up one sleeve and pulled out a small stack wrapped in a clean cloth. "I thought you might have forgotten me entirely, since you're so preoccupied with my brother."

"Nope. In my mind you'll always be the doma warrior." Her chipper reply made the man smile. He was really good-looking as well, especially when he smiled. She immediately began thinking about who to introduce him to when the women came on board. Larok's brother seemed nice. It would be a waste not to hook him up. A simple introduction wasn't meddling was it?

Larok smiled down at her as she munched on a wafer. "Like me, you have a keen sense of smell, my queen."

"Yes, we're the perfect pair. Now, let's get going before

they leave us behind. We got that bedding down thing to get back to, remember?"

Using humor to cover her anxiety was a bad habit. Power walking to the loading bay, Hope steeled herself for what was to come. No matter what she found on that ship, she was not going to freak out or leave anyone behind.

HOPE

THE TRIP FROM THE *OBSIDIAN* TO THE RAIDER'S SHIP crept slowly by. The shielding the shuttles used to mask their arrival was thrown out of sync if the craft moved too quickly. Draconian shuttles were sleek, modern, and fast. Hope supposed the speed would come in handy when they were making their getaway.

The mission started much like Larok had said it would, with their large elite warriors climbing through the docking ring onto the enemy vessel first. Larok followed, and Hope came up last. They put a fancy biometric lock on the docking ring to ensure nothing crawled into their shuttle in their absence and headed for the loading bay where the women were being held.

The rescue party encountered some resistance in the corridor right outside the loading bay. Hope crouched behind a bulkhead, while the elite warriors had a bit of a shootout with the squids. Laser fire ripped back and forth as Larok covered her with his armor-clad body. That was all kinds of unnecessary, since she was wearing the same armor. However, Hope was not foolish enough to start an argument over something so inconsequential; instead she let it roll right over her. No sense distracting him even for a second while on a dangerous mission, she thought.

The worst part so far, in Hope's opinion, was climbing over dead squid bodies. Something made the squids partially disintegrate at death, so instead of slimy but firm bodies, they were piles of slime and squid-jelly. Even through her armored and climate-controlled mask, they stank. The squid-smell took her back to her time in the cages with the women, and her body was overcome by shaking. The hot prickle of tears crept into her eyes. Hope stopped for one second—all the time she had—to remind herself that the mission was to rescue all her friends from the cages and that awful stink.

The rescuers eventually made their way to the loading bay. For Hope, the mission was riddled with one difficulty after another. Hope felt herself rising from the floor before she could manage to hold onto anything to keep herself down. Larok grabbed her by the ankle, pulled her back down, and turned on her magnetic boots by hitting a button on the inside of each boot. Resisting the urge to facepalm herself, she realized why the warriors had been tapping their boots together that way.

Larok looked down at her with a bit of a frown on his face. "One tap activates the boots. Two taps lowers the magnetic pull. Once activated, stomping your foot will increase the magnetic pull. You will need to adjust it yourself, as it is set for the body weight of an average young warrior."

Dodging out of the way of a levitating pile of stinky squid gel, she quipped, "Thanks for the heads up. I appreciate it." Everything about this day was surreal.

"Our warriors will make re-establishing artificial gravity

a priority. It will happen fast, so avoid being caught under anything dangerous or gross." The thought of a slimy squid body landing on top of her, caused bile to rise in her throat. Nodding, she watched him move forward to work with the other warriors who were disabling the locking mechanisms on the loading bay door with their laser weapons. When the outer covering was damaged, they ripped out handfuls of glowing filaments until the doors popped open.

Holstering their weapons, the elite warriors grabbed the bottom of the bay door and flew straight up into the air, forcing the door open enough for them to enter. The elites flew right into the middle of the room and pounced on the two squid men standing guard. Hope glanced at Larok. "We don't fire our weapons in enclosed areas where queens might be damaged."

Just then the gravity slammed back on. It felt like suddenly being fitted with a heavy backpack after the few moments of feeling light as a feather. She bent down to hit the button on her boots until the magnetic feeling went away. Unsure how she managed it, Hope made a mental note to get more training on the uniform if they made it out alive.

She went to Larok and whispered. "Are our warriors okay?"

"One was stabbed in the arm, but I suspect he will be fine. Talk to the queens, my Hope. Make them understand that we are not their enemies."

Shoving up off the floor, she ran into the middle of the room. All the women had pressed themselves back against the wall but surged forward when they saw her. The warriors got to work busting the locks on each cage. It was happening so fast, they were bewildered when the warriors moved on instead of yanking them out of the cages like the squid men usually did.

Taking a deep breath, Hope announced, "My old friends! I brought my new friends to rescue you! Remember when the squids sent me out to die? I was rescued by a Draconian vessel, and they agreed to come here at great risk to set you free."

Glancing down at a very dead squid guy melting on the floor, she added, "Not that it turned out to be much of a risk. We have shuttles waiting to ferry you back to their ship."

Instead of moving, they stood gaping at her. "Come on, snap out of it, ladies. The quicker we get off the ship, the quicker I can pull the warriors back from the fight. I don't want to risk them anymore than I have to."

Shoving the door to her cage open, Ella rushed over to her with Stacy right on her heels. "You always said Draconians were the good guys."

Grinning at her friend, Hope asked, "Are you ready to bust outta this joint?"

"Well, I've been working on an ingenious plan of my own, but since you're here, I'll hitch a ride with you and the hot warriors."

"I've already called dibs on the hottie covering our six at the bay door. Don't worry there are about a thousand of them on the mother ship."

The other women began slowing coming forward.

Ella asked curiously. "How did you get a mother ship?"

Slapping her playfully on the shoulder, Hope responded, "It's a long story and we don't have time to talk. Let's get the hell outta here, and I'll tell you all about it when we're safe."

Kalar stopped by for a minute to run a medical scanner

over Ella and Stacy. "You are dehydrated and malnourished."

Ella frowned at him. "And dirty and tired and about done with being run over by pushy men who can't even say hello before they begin shoving machines in our faces."

Moving the scanner out of her face, he stepped back. "My apologies, little queen."

Ella shifted her attention back to Hope. "We're really just going to walk out of here?"

"You are going to walk outta here. I'm staying. For some reason they have about thirty women being held in a secondary location. We're going to make our way there and we'll meet you on the *Obsidian*."

"Cool name for a ship."

"If you make it there first, ask for Tamen. He's the one I put in charge of making preparations for all of you. They have a huge, spa-like room where you can bathe, get clean clothing and some food. Keep everyone together and organized. I'll come as soon as I can."

"I'll do what I can, Hope. You know how women are. It's like herding cats."

Grinning at Ella, she stated sincerely. "You'll be fine. Step up and take charge! God knows, the warriors will do whatever you ask of them. Just be nice. We owe them our lives."

"Will do. Stay safe out there, girl."

Hope and Larok waited until several shuttles had docked one right after another and all the women were away. Then they linked up with a small team of warriors and made their way across the ship. No sooner had they started moving than the ship rocked under their feet. Larok spun on his heel to steady her. Hope collided right into his strong arms. "Let me guess, that was your old man taking out the weapons array, so they can't fire on the shuttles?"

"My father always follows the plan. He drilled into us repeatedly how dangerous it is for warriors to operate independently in a crisis. Our unity is our strength."

"Well I say, 'if it ain't broke, don't fix it.'"

When the ship went quiet, they continued moving closer to the bay where the few remaining women were being held. It was slow going because they met resistance at every turn. The warriors were smart, though. Their fighting style involved fighters at specific vantage points working in unison. They brought down squid after squid, more than Hope even thought were on board.

When they busted through the door, she was face to

face with the one she'd named Head Squid Dude in her mind. His face contorted into an expression of disbelief and fury. He pointed one long tentacle at her and said something unintelligible. Larok stepped between her and the alien spewing nonsense. "Is he the one who left the marks on your arm?"

"Yes. He's the one in charge of this ship."

Without hesitation, Larok lifted his weapon and aimed for the squid's head. Upon discharging his weapon, they were shocked to see the laser fire being absorbed into some kind of protective shielding. Frustrated chirps sounded from the warriors, as they all concentrated their weapons fire on the shielding, hoping to bring it down.

One lone female voice rang out from the cage. "You have to destroy the energy buffer."

Hope asked, "What's that?"

"Jesus, it's the big black box on the left. Don't you know anything about the Zelerians?"

Glancing over at the young redhead, Hope shouted back, "Not one damn thing, kid."

The warriors trained their weapons on the energy buffer, ignoring the women entirely. After multiple coordinated blasts, the box was still intact, and Head Squid Dude was preening.

Larok's anxious voice called out. "My queen, use your heirloom weapon."

Knowing that he could only be referring to the tiny pistol, Hope pulled it from its holster and aimed towards the black box. Swallowing hard, she pulled the trigger, lighting up the entire space. When the flash of blinding white light subsided, Hope stood gaping at the empty space where the box had been. There was now huge hole in the metal wall, making the room beyond clearly visible. Lowering her shaking hand, Hope took a deep breath and shoved the pistol back into place.

The moment the shield deactivated with a loud pop, Larok stepped forward to mete out Draconian justice to the crusty raider. Instead, they watched a strange warrior appear behind the squid. He was wearing some kind of formsuit that enabled him to blend seamlessly into the background of the room. Powering a blade through the squid's head, he ripped it halfway down his body with very little effort.

After dispatching the alien, the warrior turned to the cage full of women. "You are safe now, Sin. These people have come to rescue us. They are the ones I saw on the monitor fighting their way to this part of the ship."

"I've never been so happy to see a Draconian before in my life."

The warrior busied himself cleaning his blade. The young woman grabbed the bars of the cage. "Umm, Vxion, can you please get me the hell out of here?"

"You should not be cursing. Your parents would not approve." Stalking over to the cage, he pried the lock off with the hilt of his short sword. It had the face of a dragon with its mouth open on the end. The warrior used it as a claw to twist the lock off. He jerked the door open, and gestured for her to come out.

She flew to his side, giving him a hug and a chaste kiss on the cheek. "Thanks, I owe you one." Turning to Hope, her face lit up. "Are we blowing this popsicle stand? My parents are going to lose their minds. I'm of age, but that doesn't keep them from trying to micromanage every area of my life."

Hope took a few steps closer to the young woman. "I've got some really bad news for you."

"Worse than being abducted by aliens from an amusement park on a Taladar moon base?"

"A hundred times worse than that, I'm afraid."

Making a come-hither gesture with her fingers, the scrappy girl muttered. "Bring it on, sister. I'm outta my cage and ready to fight."

Larok stepped forward to face the one identified as Vxion, his lip curled back. "What are you?" Hope cringed at how inappropriate that question was. People in civilized space didn't just roll up on people that way.

The girl stepped between them. "Don't talk to my friend like that. He's been the only thing standing between us and certain death."

Hope moved forward, staring at the young woman. Her warrior had called her Sin. It must be short for something. "You look so familiar." She had little ridges along her temples. It was the only feature indicating an alien heritage.

Stepping back against her warrior, her eyes slid away. "I'm no one of note."

It hit Hope hard and fast who the young lady was, and it popped out before she could censor herself. "You're the daughter of that Yuroba rebel leader." Searching her mind, she finally pulled the information from the dark recesses of her mind. "Sinthia Scarlock, as I live and breathe. Sweet day in the morning, what are you doing out in the black? If you're planning a takeover of this sector of space, you're biting off way more than you can chew."

Rolling her eyes, the woman asked, "Even I couldn't manage to establish a stronghold capable of taking over an entire sector of space, from inside that damned cage."

"Well I thought it might be some clever ploy where they thought you were their prisoner, but you were really just a mole, gathering intelligence for your rebel mother."

Shaking her head, she asked, "And who might you be?"

"Unlike you, I'm just a common scruff who signed up for the Talador bride's registry. Our ship got hit by the squids, and I got tossed out on my ass for screaming at your friends here." Gesturing to the now-dead alien, Hope huffed out an exasperated breath.

The girl eyed her back curiously. "The Zelerians don't like to be called squids. Most of them are real nice people. They visit the oceans of our home world all the time." Giving the squishy corpse of the dead captain a kick, she snarled. "Since you used it in reference to this piece of Zelerian garbage, I'll let it slide."

"It's real nice talking to you, but we need to get everyone off the ship. We'll reserve a VIP room for you and your protector."

"I'm not leaving this ship without the rest of my party. We were almost forty strong, before they separated us."

"Look kid, we already rescued them. We need to get going now."

"I want to double-check. If we left anyone behind, I'd never forgive myself."

Larok spoke up. "Our ship has scanned this vessel. You are the only ones still on board."

Vxion took her by the arm. "The Draconians are diligent in their protection of queens. If they say there are no more in need of rescue, then it is so."

Larok pulled an extra laser pistol from his side and tossed it to Vxion. "Follow the elite warriors and put your queen behind you. Her queen friends will be in the back. Our other warriors will be positioned in the rear, in case any Zelerians try to attack from behind."

"I thank you." Charging the weapon, he caught Larok's eye. "It is a good plan. Lead the way."

As they made their way back across the ship, there were groups of Zelerians lying dead on the floor around every turn, mere puddles of ooze by this point. Their stench accompanied them, of course, but this time, Hope dealt with her reaction—a little gagging, nothing more—much better. Thank goodness no dead Draconians or humans littered the areas they passed through. Hope was certain that valuing one kind of life over another made her a bad person, but she couldn't help herself.

It seemed that every able-bodied warrior was lining the corridors to see them safely through with the remaining women. Several of the Draconians were wounded, but they stubbornly stood their ground.

These alien warriors had known little in the way of freedom, caring, and respect from women, yet put themselves in harm's way to rescue them. That realization made tears sting the backs of Hope's eyes. She vowed to herself that come what may, she'd see they made it to other side. These selfless men had been dealt a raw hand in life and remained honorable and dedicated.

Finally they were pulling the seal off their docking ring, and the women were ushered into the shuttle. Unlike the one she'd met Larok on, this shuttle was spacious and held not only the group of women and their original team, but a couple dozen more warriors as well.

Staring up at the warriors who were closing off their docking ring, it occurred to her to worry about their not making it out in time. "What's going to happen to the warriors we left behind, Larok?"

"Do not worry over their safety, my queen. They are evacuating, even as we speak."

"I won't rest easy until they are all on the *Obsidian* and accounted for."

Larok's hand went to the communications unit wrapped around his ear. "I'm getting reports that our warriors have removed the wormhole device, downloaded the ship's database, and set the engines to overload. We must leave now to avoid being caught in the blast."

Sinthia grabbed him by the shirt and jerked him forward. "You can't kill every person on the ship. They're raiders, but they're still people. We can call the Intergalactic Council and have them send a retrieval team. They'll stand trial, and..."

After dislodging her hand from his clothing, Larok spoke. "Talk to the human queen, my Hope. Make her understand that the raiders refused to surrender, and there is no Intergalactic council to call. We cannot allow them to live, for if the Draconian queens learn of your world, nothing will stop them from finding a way to access it."

"What in the verse is your guy talking about?"

"I hate to say it, but my protector is correct. That bad news I was getting ready to tell you back on the raider ship is that it slipped through a wormhole in space. We're on the side with the crazy Draconian queens."

The younger woman jerked back like she's been slapped. "Well that ain't gonna work for me. They'll hunt us down if they find out we're breed-compatible with their warriors."

Hope nodded like a bobblehead doll. "That's why blowing the raider out of the sky is our only chance at keeping that secret."

"I don't like it but we can't risk them finding our dimension. There's more than just Earth at risk. Draconian queens consider any female competition and see men as slaves. My home world is teeming with Yuroba women. I won't risk them being killed or our males being subjugated."

"I wish there was another way, Sinthia."

"If there's one thing my dad taught me, it's that things are different out in the black of deep space. Sometimes you have to make tough decisions. I guess this is just the first time I've been faced with dealing death to survive."

"Welcome to my world," Hope mumbled under her breath. As the two women stared into each other's eyes, the shuttle jerked under them as it disengaged from the docking ring. Hands came out around both their waists. Vxion drew Sinthia back into his lap and secured the two of them with a safety harness. Larok did the same to Hope. The two redheads sat face-to-face, staring at each other, and for a moment it seemed they'd known each other for a very long time. Hope supposed it was the way with people who survived adversity together. It created a bond.

STANDING IN THE LOADING BAY ABOARD THE *OBSIDIAN*, Larok wrapped his arms around his new queen Hope and smelled the red strands of her hair. Together they, along with all the others, watched the raider's ship explode into a million pieces. He released a relieved breath. Since his brethren had destroyed the ship's data system after downloading the archive, the explosion would ensure nothing remained to tell any tales that the human queens had visited this dimension.

Hope sighed. "Well, now that we've dealt with the raiders, and our warriors retrieved the wormhole generator, we need to focus on figuring out a way back to Naxis."

Smoothing down her hair, Sinthia nodded. "I'm down with that idea. Do we know how to use the contraption we stole?"

Looking around at his sire and the assortment of warriors both old and young filling the bay, Larok was overcome with pride that they had managed to do the near-impossible by getting this far.

His sire spoke up. As Queen Hope's first officer, it was

his responsibility to give reports at regular intervals. "Our warriors are examining the machine and scouring through the database now, looking for clues that might enable us to better understand the process."

Being keenly interested in getting his queen to safety as soon as possible, Larok chimed in, "I remember being told of a plan to create an artificial anomaly so we could escape into free space. Why can we not use that plan to cross over?"

"Larok's right, maybe we could go with your idea." His lovely queen was eager to get back to her own sector of space.

Elder Thermon responded, "We have never tested our device, much less with real lives hanging in the balance. There are too many beings aboard this vessel to risk on unproven technology. We will use the device we know works."

Larok spoke up. "Other aliens who have accessed our sector by mistake or looking for new trading partners were not rewarded for their curiosity. I believe they learned quickly that Exion space is to be avoided at all costs, for our queens conquer rather than trade. It is a worry that they came here at all."

"We are focusing our effort on learning how to operate the device and rekey it to exit into the Naxis sector," Elder Thurmon said to Larok. Then he raised his voice to announce to all, "I would like to remind our new visitors that we have contamination protocols in place aboard this vessel. Everyone must follow proper medical safety proto-cols." Turning to Vxion, he continued. "Our preliminary scans on the shuttle picked up some irregularities in your biology."

"I am unique."

Larok frowned. "You look less humanoid than any male I have ever encountered."

Stilling himself, Vxion's skin began to shift, making him look extremely humanoid.

"You are a shifter. We have heard of beings that can subtly shift their appearance to resemble other alien species, but I thought it was a myth."

Sinthia sounded off. "Hey, my friend isn't some kind of show-and-tell project. Leave him alone."

"We are just trying to understand, young queen."

Sinthia head whipped around to Elder Thermon. "No you weren't. You're being nosey and making him feel like he has to prove something to you. For the record, he doesn't." Rolling her eyes, she explained. "He just has more control of his muscles and can shift them around slightly. There's nothing nefarious going on here."

"How did you come to know him? Was Vxion born on your home world?"

"In a manner of speaking. He's lived with us my entire life. Not that it's any of your business, but we do everything together, much like other siblings."

Hope cut into their escalating disagreement. "If our warriors haven't seen anything like your brother before, we'll need to give him the once-over. Before you get your panties in a twist, they medically scanned all of us, so we're not asking anything of him that we haven't been willing to do ourselves."

"Fine, but I want to be there when it happens."

Larok's father tried to get ahold of the conversation again. "It will take us some time to process the information from the raider's databanks and formulate a plan of action. I should point out that our activities are being monitored by the other queens on long-range scanners. They aren't close enough to scan individual people, but blowing up the raider wouldn't have gone unnoticed," Jeron finished.

Hope reached out to slip her hand into Larok's. "Why do I get the feeling that you have more bad news?"

"Your words are truer than you think. Unfortunately, the raider managed to find a moon worthy of being harvested to hide behind."

"I don't understand what that means, Jeron."

Larok's sire tried to explain in terms the human queens could understand. "A harvest-rich planet is teeming with minerals, gemstones and precious metals. Draconian queens harvest these resources by hitting the planet with a particle weapon."

"Won't that destroy the stuff you want to harvest?"

"We have a fruit on our home world. It is round with a tough exterior shell. Delivering a forceful impact to the point of weakness, the exterior fractures causing round pebbles of sweet fruit to be released."

"We have fruit similar to that on Earth. It takes a little more effort to open but small beads of tart, juicy fruit are extracted."

"The particle weapon does much the same to a planet or moon. Our warriors peruse the wreckage in shuttles specially outfitted to harvest different types of resources. Not many people know that deep inside a planet the density of desirable materials is much greater and increased in size."

"And what am I missing?"

"The weapon produces elevated radiation levels for a short time following the explosion, making the harvest a dirty, thankless and dangerous task."

"Absolutely not, Jeron. We have a medical bay full of

warriors wounded in battle. We aren't going to put more in harm's way for the sake of a mining operation."

The older man frowned. Larok provided more information to help his new queen understand their situation. "Draconian queens covet these resources beyond all things in the 'verse. No queen in her right mind would pass up an opportunity to harvest a rich planet. Now that we have drawn the attention of the other queens to the planet, they will become suspicious if we do not follow through with a harvest, especially as the planet is rich in Nalisite. It is rare and used to reinforce our outer hull."

Sinthia leaned over. "Your warriors speak the truth. Nalisite is extremely valuable. I agree that putting lives in danger to collect it is wrong. We can have the warriors drag their feet, waiting until the radiation drops to safe levels. I would also request that Vxion and I be allowed to participate in the harvest. Few Yuroba vessels can have Nalisite for their hulls. It leaves us vulnerable."

"Let the warriors harvest it, and we'll give you..." Hope said.

"That is not done by our people. Charity is for the weak. Reward follows risk. It's humiliating enough that I allowed myself to be abducted from a pleasure planet. Not being thought of as strong enough to engage in a simple mining operation would remove me from the line of succession."

"You're barely eighteen."

"I've been of age among the Yuroba since I was fifteen. I've been mining off and on since I was twelve. I need this win to balance things out."

His queen reluctantly agreed. "Fine kid, just be careful. I don't want your parents on my case if things go bad."

"Things are not going to go bad. It's my job to see that they don't," Vxion said.

Commander Jeron interjected diplomatically, "We are in agreement to proceed?"

"So far we've been discussing if we have the capacity. I need us to focus on the ethics of what we're doing for a second. We're talking about blowing an entire planet out of existence, destroying every living thing. What if there are intelligent life forms on it?"

Jeron responded, "It has none, my queen."

Looking at him, she gestured imploringly. "Think of all the plant and animal life we'd be wiping out of existence. Maybe we'd be eliminating their chance to evolve into sentient beings."

Elder Thermon chanced joining the conversation once more. "Scans of the moon reveal no life forms. There is no water, and the surface temperatures preclude it from being a place where life could possibly exist."

Hope dropped her arms, wringing her hands in her lap. "What kind of impact would destroying the moon have on the planet it orbits?"

Larok had to admit his queen was a fighter.

Elder Thermon answered respectfully. "The moon affects the tilt of the planet in relation to its orbit around the sun, increasing the tilt somewhat. Without the moon, the degree of the tilt would be less extreme. The degree the planet tilts causes seasons, with a more extreme tilt causing the seasons to be more extreme. If we destroy the moon, aside from the bits that strike the planet, it will just mean the seasons are more temperate. Most of the flying debris will get burned up in the planet's atmosphere."

Jeron verbalized his agreement. "That was my assessment as well, Queen Hope. The planet is teeming with plant and animal life but no intelligent life forms. I believe it is worth the risk for three reasons. Destroying the moon would have little impact on the planet it orbits. It will keep the other queens from coming to investigate. Most importantly, gathering the resources may make a difference in our ability to survive once we get to Naxis space. I have no intention of showing up on our new home world with hungry warriors and nothing to contribute. It would be most unseemly."

Elder Thermon added, "There is also a slim possibility that your Queen Cassandra will not offer us sanctuary on the new home world. If that is the case, we will need the stones to trade for food and fuel until we can locate a new home world."

Shaking her head, his queen finally capitulated. "I know what you say is true. I don't want to take a chance on taking all of you to free space without a safety net or our getting targeted by the other ships in this sector of space."

His sire asked, "Do we have your permission to proceed, Queen Hope?"

"Of course, Jeron. Just be really careful with the warriors. I don't want to lose any in a mining operation. That would be such a waste of life."

"I will ensure they wait until the last possible moment to enter the debris field, so as much of the radiation as possible will have dissipated."

"Make sure they are all wearing protective armor, and the shields are operating at full capacity on the shuttles."

"I will see it done." His sire shot him a level look. "I believe your queen could use some rest while we prepare for our next mission and attempt to get the wormhole generator working."

As usual, his queen had other ideas. "Thanks for

looking out for me, Jeron. However, I would prefer to check on my friends. They're probably all kinds of worried about what's going on."

The younger queen also spoke up. "I want to see my friends as well. I can't believe that accepting an invitation to celebrate my birthday got them all abducted."

Hope reached out to the younger queen, locking arms together, they moved towards the exit. "I'd love to hear about how the squid dudes, I mean Zelerians . . ."

Following along behind them Larok listened to the tale of the young queens frolicking on the pleasure planet for the day and visiting a remote lagoon to relax and watch the sunset.

Sinthia's voice became more exasperated the longer she spoke of her abduction. "A man dressed as a pleasure host kneeled and slid some large pellets into the edge of the lagoon. We thought it was a fancy medicinal thing or maybe something to make bubbles. He looked so harmless that it didn't set off any warning bells in my head."

"Let me guess, it was something to knock you out?"

"Not hardly, why risk our drowning ourselves when they could make us drowsy and unable to fight back? Zelerians have an amphibian heritage. If you think they're strong out of the water, that's nothing compared to the raw power they wield in their natural environment. None of us stood a chance."

"I've had it out with one of them. They're all tentacles and muscle in a fight."

"It might have been a different story if I'd been armed. Unfortunately, there's nowhere to stick a gun when you're wearing a bikini."

The translation program was drawing images in Larok's mind of a very tiny set of under clothing. He tried to imagine his Hope wearing such a garment. He asked Vxion quietly, "Why did you not protect your queen?"

"Pleasure planets are renowned for being safe havens. Sinthia sent me away in order that they might have female time together. Since this is a common occurrence, I acquired the services of a pleasure female to give me a massage. When it came time to retrieve them, they were nowhere to be found."

"I suppose you tracked them to the Zelerian vessel."

"Yes. I realized there were too many females to rescue only after the ship had broken orbit. It is a mistake I will not make again."

Larok waved his hand over the scanning plate when they approached the huge queen chambers for the rescued queens. The conversation never faltered once between the two queens. It made him suspicious that social interaction strategies were an important part of the core training on their home world.

HOPE

Rolling into the queen's chamber, Hope searched the sea of faces for the women she'd grown close to during her captivity. In doing so, she noticed they were all clean and many were eating and drinking. They were being attended to by Draconians dressed in the long flowing pants Kala had worn earlier that morning instead of regular uniform like the rest of the crew. Everyone seemed to be in good spirits.

Sinthia zoomed around her and headed for a group of younger women. She vaguely recognized them as the companions she'd seen in the cage of younger women. Her friend Vxion followed close behind, looking for all the world like he belonged at her side.

A familiar voice rang out of the menagerie of women and warriors. "Hope, you made it! We were starting to get worried about you."

Spying Stacy and Ella sitting in a small group in one of the seating areas, she headed in their direction. Instead of walking with her to join her and her friends, Larok tried to slip into position along the wall with some other warriors.

Around the perimeter of the room were about thirty warriors standing guard motionlessly. Now, why in the 'verse would they do a thing like that? Spinning on her heel, she walked straight over to him. He stepped out to meet her.

"You need something, my Hope?"

Swallowing down her annoyance, she tried to find the words to communicate how absurd it was for warriors to stand guard in a perfectly safe environment. "I was wondering if we could modify the manner in which warriors guard over us while we're aboard your vessel."

"We would welcome ideas on how to ensure the queens feel more comfortable among us."

"Well, we really don't care for warriors that don't mix and mingle. I realize it might be more complicated, but we'd appreciate it if they could come off the wall and introduce themselves. Humans place more trust in people we know."

A nearby warrior spoke up. "Several queens have approached us, but we thought it better to leave their care to those trained to meet their needs."

"That thought makes sense. However, if women are approaching you, it's probably because they're attracted to you. Or maybe they desire a nonromantic friendship. I would suggest that you take some time to get to know them before you reject their advances out of hand."

Several of the males made irritated chirping sounds. Hope knew it was because she suggested their behavior could be seen as rejecting. Larok stared down at her for a brief moment before speaking. "Do as our new queen asks, my brethren. Queen Hope would never lead us astray."

The warriors reluctantly moved forward and dispersed awkwardly throughout the room. "I think my brethren hardly know how to converse with a queen."

Grabbing Larok's hand, she murmured, "You figured it out. They will as well."

As they walked across the room, he asked curiously. "Why are you so persistent in this matter, my Hope?"

"They're wasting a good opportunity to be noticed and perhaps chosen to get to know a woman. They can guard and mingle. Those are not mutually exclusive activities. It's better that way, especially since there is no real danger aboard this vessel."

As they approached, one of her queen friends spoke. "What was that all about? We've been trying to get them to come off the walls since we sat down here."

"When I first arrived, they were doing the same thing. It's standard operating procedure for Draconian warriors. They're also probably being a little hypervigilant about safety after everything we've been through."

"Well, they've been pretty great. I can't tell you how happy I am to be clean, fed, and out of danger."

"You might want to scratch that last item off your list, at least for now."

"I heard we blew up the squid ship. We all assumed that we were on our way back home."

"You should sit down for this one." Hope dropped onto the end of a seating platform and waited while other women crowded around.

Calen horned in beside Larok, looking worried. "What is the purpose of telling your queen friends about our situation? I believe such knowledge will simply worry them unnecessarily."

Before Hope could respond, Larok spoke. "We should not interfere in the business of queens, for we know little of the rules human queens live by, Calen. Perhaps they are required by law to share such information."

"Their social rules are difficult to understand, as they bear little resemblance to the adversarial ways of the queens we have known."

Ella's eyes lifted to Calen. "Humans consider withholding information about their safety to be a grievous offense."

Calen's eyes grew perfectly round, but he kept his lips sealed. Hope couldn't tell whether his reaction was because a woman had spoken to him directly or because he might have come across as being disrespectful.

Hope cleared her throat and began explaining to the human queens that they were now in the wrong sector of space. She carefully explained about how the science team was trying to install the stolen wormhole generator and then started talking about the harvest. Her monologue was punctuated with questions from the other women. When it was all said and done, they were deeply concerned but not freaking out.

As the crowd began to dissipate, Stacy moved closer. "Now tell me the real scoop. Is that all that's going on?"

Hope grinned at her mischievous friend. "Good God woman, isn't that enough for you?"

"Yea, it's more than enough. I can't seem to calm down, and I'm going a little stir crazy in this room. Are we allowed to leave the room?"

Shrugging, Hope replied, "From what I can tell, women can do pretty much whatever they want. The men around these parts only object if you are somehow putting yourself in danger."

"That's exactly what I wanted to hear. Now about the nuts and bolts of getting a man, how exactly does that piece work?"

Hope opened her mouth and closed it again. Shooting

Larok a questioning look, she asked demurely. "How does that work, exactly? The guys are a little standoffish."

"Much like it did with us."

"I'm a little cloudy on how that went down. You rescued me, we talked and ended up flirting with each other and then we were officially together."

"I made the human flirt only after you made the mating gesture to me. No warrior would do so before, because it would seem like we were pressing ourselves upon a queen. You bared your teeth to me in the traditional gesture of courtship. I in turn, was careful to reciprocate your many gestures until you selected me."

Hope couldn't help but smile at his description of how they got close. "I don't remember baring my teeth at you, babe."

"You do so most every time you look at me. In fact, you are doing it even now."

Shock exploded in Hope's chest as she realized what he was referring to. "We have to full-on smile so you can see our teeth. Is that the mating gesture you are referring to?"

"You smile a lot, but mostly only show your teeth to me."

She pulled him down beside her and murmured, "I'll be more careful about that in the future. We wouldn't want other men to get the wrong impression."

Stacy perked up. "That's what cues them to warm up to us? Sorry, but I have to go spread the word."

As the few remaining people drifted away, Hope turned to her handsome drone. "So are there any more secrets you want to share with me about mating?"

"About mating? No."

His cryptic answer only more curious about him. "How about secrets related to you?"

His eyes slid away, and he made a move to stand. Keeping her hold on his hand, she kept him in place. "Is this a good secret or a bad secret?"

"It is a very bad one, my Hope."

"Are you going to tell me what it is?"

"Not unless you command me to do so."

"You don't trust me with your secrets."

"You are a queen."

Taking a moment to think it over, she came to a quick decision. "I'm not giving you any more commands. If and when you want to share your terrible secret, come to me, and we'll talk it out."

Larok's shoulders relaxed, and the big brute's horns sprang back up slightly. He was relieved. Hope knew that in other circumstances, she'd be highly offended by his lack of trust. However, they'd only known each other a short time, and he grew up in an environment where women were devious, unbalanced and downright vicious at times. He would have had to have been very guarded around them to survive. Given all that, she honestly wasn't taking his reluctance to share all his deepest secrets personally. He was a person deeply in need of love and understanding. Who was she to force the poor man to do anything?

Rubbing his arm gently, she murmured, "Want to get out of here and find a nice quiet place to nest for the night?"

His head came up, and she saw the surprised expression on his face. "You still wish to share your bed with me, even though I have displeased you?"

"Has it ever once occurred to you that you have a right to privacy?"

Swallowing thickly, he nodded. "Until now it seemed like a futile wish."

"It's been a long day. Let's worry about all that complicated stuff later."

"Come, my Hope. I will take you to a small chamber where we can shut out everyone and everything for a cycle of rest."

"Small sounds really nice and intimate."

Standing, his lips curled up into a smile. "I like this human word, intimate. We have no such word in our language to describe emotional closeness between a queen and a warrior." Tugging her to her feet, he began leading her across the room. Hope passed Calen, who still had the scared-stiff expression clamped tightly in place. Ella turned in time for Hope to see her full-on smile. That woman was definitely interested in staking a claim. Hope worried if now was the best time to be distracting the warriors with courting.

LAROK LED HIS CURIOUS NEW QUEEN TO A TINY chamber normally reserved for breeding males. There were several dozen such rooms scattered over the ship, since ship designers normally just placed them in areas that were too small to be useful for any other purpose. They had little more than a cleansing room and a larger sleeping platform. Both features were of benefit to a breeding male. The larger platform in particular, provided for his comfort.

"Wow, this place is tiny."

"My brethren would be upset to know I brought you to a place so far beneath the dignity of a queen."

Looking up at him, she smiled. "Well, they can all go worry about some other gal. The only thing that matters is if you and I are comfortable here. We're only sleeping. The bed is big enough for two. I just want a quick misting and some cuddling. How about you?"

"I wish for more."

Pulling her bottom lip from between her teeth, his queen immediately made the mating gesture. It felt more potent now the she was fully aware of the meaning behind the gesture. "I thought warriors didn't have the right of choosing."

The sweet laughing tone of her voice and the look on her face told him she was teasing him. Pulling open his uniform, he peeled it down his torso. Reaching for her, he responded playfully. "You have taught me that perhaps males should speak their mind. How else will our queens learn to please us?" Those were the most brazen words Larok had ever spoken in his life. He waited breathlessly for his queen to respond.

"I am interested in pleasing you. You know that, don't you?"

"I thought maybe I was confusing what I wished with what is possible where you come from." Relaxing a little, he began remove his queen's clothing in preparation for a proper cleansing.

"I might be interested in a little more. What did you have in mind?"

"Perhaps after we cleanse, we can practice making the human kiss. I wish to be proficient when our time of breeding arrives."

"Come on, you old smooth talker. Let's cleanse each other, and we'll see about some lip locking afterwards."

A thrill ran up Larok's spine at the thought of rubbing cleansing foam into his precious queen. Had any warrior ever been offered such an opportunity? The thought of touching her soft skin made his mating scent rise. Automatically taking a deep breath, he quelled his base instincts to mate. When she turned to walk into the cleansing room, the sight of her naked form and long fire-colored strands bouncing against her back sent a sharp stab of lust coursing through his body. Seeing her pert backside reminded him of the sight of her struggling to get off the cleansing unit the evening before. His mouth watered at the thought of tasting her soft pink center.

Losing the battle to control his mating instincts, he quickly followed her in an effort to wash off the mating scent that was surely going to swamp them if he wasn't careful. Turning on the mister, he shoved one head up to the height of his shoulder and the other down to his waist. Hope stepped forward and turned to him, dipping her head backwards into the soft mist being sprayed from the unit. Her body was lovely, curvy and a delicate pink.

"You're staring, babe. Better get under the mister so I can soap you up."

Stepping back like she requested, he glanced down to see his mating member had readied for breeding. It was an embarrassing reminder that he had failed to control himself in the presence of a queen. Then again, what warrior could be expected to do so when faced with such an arousing sight. Larok watched his queen's eyes drift over his body, lingering on his prominent offering. She seemed anything but disapproving. He reached down to touch himself. Drawing his hand roughly over his thickness drew her immediate notice. His wings burst out, bumping into the sides of the cleansing unit.

Suddenly, she was moving towards him. He stepped forward to meet her, so the mister was spraying on both their backs. His wings loosened a bit, as the mist gathered along the thin bands running along each joint.

Pulling some foam from the dispenser on the wall, he rubbed his hands together and began with her shoulders. Drawing her forward slightly, he ran his hands over her shoulders, down her back and grasped a fleshy globe in each hand. Lifting her slightly, he made the human kiss with her.

A soft moan escaped from her lips a moment before her

hands twined around his neck. As he delved his tongue in to explore the one who had chosen him above all others, her hands began to move, exploring the ridges running up the back of his neck and finally grasping each horn in a small hand. The next thing he knew she was gently stroking his stiff horns like he'd stroked his rod.

"You press me to my limits this day, little queen."

Answering breathlessly as her lips moved on him again, she said, "That's me, testing limits is kind of my thing in life."

Easing her off his body, Larok stepped back to rinse the cleansing foam off. She did the same. The moment they were clean, he hit the dryer, and they finger-combed her long red strands again. Bending down, he picked her up and walked to the sleeping platform. This time his queen did not protest being in his arms. Instead, she laid her head on his chest and caressed his arm with one hand.

Larok felt empowered that the lovely queen was open to his boldness. Coming down beside her, he asked, "What do you wish of me, my queen?"

"Maybe for starters you could just call me Hope when we're alone together."

Running a small bunch of her strands through his fingers, he murmured, "Your strands are delicate and soft."

"We call it hair."

"There is no hair among any of the species we have encountered in Exion space. We find it very beautiful. Maybe our little ones will have hair."

"If they do, it will probably be red like mine."

"That would please me greatly."

"I'd like them to have wings and your nice blue skin tone."

Dropping the strand he ran the backs of two fingers along her collar bone. "Pink is nice."

Capturing his hand, she pulled it down to cover one of her soft rounded globes. It fit perfectly in his palm and the tip became firm when he touched it. "I noticed that touching your horns was arousing for you."

His eyes lifted from her chest to her eyes. "Draconian warriors are sensitive there."

"Want to know where human women are sensitive?"

Gently fingering the darker pink area, he responded, "You are sensitive here, I think. When I touch you like this, you move closer to me and your breathing changes."

"You're learning all my secrets."

Rolling the tip between two fingers, he observed, "You are very pliant."

"Although being described as pliant is true, it not as arousing as you might think."

"Our queens do not have soft mounds like this. Their chests are flat like a warrior's."

"They must not nurse their young."

Larok jerked back slightly. "Human females feed their young? I have noticed this in other species." Wrapping his hand around her soft globe, he tested it with a slight squeeze. "What part of the mating process triggers the nourishment to come?"

Frowning slightly, she responded, "I guess giving birth."

"Our queens do not give birth."

Looking up at him, she smiled. "Now that you mention it, I remember reading about how that works. I believe humans have given birth to Draconian babies and Draconian males do the hatching thing. I remember seeing an image of a breeding male. He had a long line stretching across his lower abdomen. It looked like a small string of pearls just below the surface of his skin."

"He must have been a true breeder. We have a seam that opens for the eggs to be removed. I will only have one or two small eggs, instead of a string. It is why I was not selected to be a breeder."

Cupping his face in one hand, she looked into his eyes. "I'll let you in on a little secret. Most human women don't want dozens of kids all at the same time. That's a little overwhelming. We prefer to have one or two, sometimes three at a time. We consider that a lot of kids to keep up with. If we had more than that, it would hard to ensure each got enough of our time to feel loved."

"That sounds wise. Our females, wish ten times that many and for their breeders to be continuous breeding."

"That sounds like a lot to expect out of a man."

"We are accustomed to bowing to the wishes of our queens."

"How about we turn that custom upside down for one night?"

Unable to keep the excitement off his face, Larok asked, "You wish for this one night to bow to my wishes?"

Nodding, she replied, "Why not? You seem like a guy with pretty good judgement. I liked your being in charge when we showered."

Eyeing her suspiciously, Larok asked, "Queens do not yield power for no reason. What do you hope to gain by doing so?"

"Nothing in particular, I just think it would be fun to switch up the power dynamic. I'm not comfortable always having to be in charge when we're alone together."

Larok's wings rustled at the thought of having his way with such an accommodating queen. "You give yourself over to me, allowing me to touch and taste your body as I like?"

"I'd really like that."

Intent on enjoying her undivided attention for as long as it would last, he moved back to get a better look and to consider what he wanted most this night.

LAROK

LAROK'S POSSESSIVE DRAGON INSTINCTS FLARED. HE backed up off the bed and stood staring at Hope, his wings slowly coming out on each side of his massive shoulders. He wanted this human female so badly his manhood pointed up to his stomach and he noticed her staring.

Interrupting her questing eyes, he spoke firmly. "I wish to see all that the gods have given you, my queen."

The queen responded by running her hands down to cover her queenly treasures. Since her legs were closed, it was clear he was being denied. "I thought you were going to start using my name when we're alone together,"

"I command you to open your legs so that I might see what blessings you have to share with your consort. Will you submit to my wishes, Hope?"

Chewing her bottom lip, she nodded. Removing her hands, she allowed her legs to drop open, once again displaying her moist center to his eager eyes. She was just as lovely as he remembered. Above the exquisite pink parts, she had a small triangle of short strands to match the ones on her head. It was nothing Larok expected, but it was incredibly arousing. Stepping forward, he flapped his wings and landed with his face cradled between her thighs.

"I wish to taste you here. What say you, Hope?"

"I'd say that sounds pretty amazing. Careful of the sharp teeth, though."

"It will be as you wish."

It was funny that the pretty human worried about getting her delicate bits mangled by his sharp teeth. Larok had more sense than to injure her, especially in such a sensitive area. Using both hands he explored her body. Being so close was interfering with his ability to think rationally. Her scent clung to his fingers, begging his tongue to taste. He leaned forward and swiped his tongue along the pale pink valley that beckoned him. Her essence reminded him of a flower that grew in profusion by the oceans of his home planet. Taking his time, he let his tongue explore every crease, and he discovered where her queenly juices were the thickest.

Hope was squirming and produced soft sounds that only a queen would make, clearly loving his gentle ministrations. Larok's tongue bumped into a tiny nub near the top of her sex. Each time he touched it, his queen reacted. This must be her sweet spot, perhaps the equivalent of stroking his horns. Teasing her with his tongue in several different ways, he discovered that drawing the tiny nub into his mouth and sucking it elicited the biggest reaction. Suddenly, her entire body was shaking, and sweet nectar coated his tongue. Leaving off the little nub, he chased down every drop.

"Oh, wow, that was pretty damned incredible, babe."

He crawled up her body and found his reward in her beautiful green eyes. "You taste better than doma."

She let out a tiny laugh. It was light and delightful to his ear, like a little chime. Larok was amazed at how easily the little human queens could work their way into a warrior's affections. Looking down at her, he wondered how far he would go to keep her underneath him. What he would do to keep her with him. It scared him to realize how attached he was becoming to her.

Shoving all that from his mind, he captured her lips in a searing kiss. Again, she moved closer and clung to him. Having her in his arms was the single most pleasurable experience of his life.

Her hand drifted down to his throbbing rod. "What were you planning to do with this?"

"I think you know how a warrior and a queen's body fit together."

"How would you feel about me putting my mouth there, like you just did for me?"

Larok felt his nostrils flare, and a spike of lust hit so hard it was painful. "Our queens do not do such things. It is forbidden."

"I suppose in a culture where males take, and females accept, tending to a warrior that way is frowned upon. Forget about everything you were taught. Do you wish to experience that kind of pleasure or not?"

Larok answered without hesitation. "I wish it."

"You're in charge. Command me to do it, and I will."

"You wish it as well?"

"Oh yeah, I want it a lot."

Leaning back on his hands, he intoned, "Pleasure me with your warm wet tongue. I demand that you satisfy me as I have you, my sweet."

"I have to say, I am loving all the equality going on tonight, babe."

He watched as she came to her knees and reached out to grasp his thick member. "I like the way you look."

Dropping a kiss onto the tip, she began to paint his heated flesh with her delightfully soft tongue. His arms began shaking beneath him as the pleasure became almost unbearable. It was overwhelming him, making it difficult to breathe, much less think clearly. An unpleasant thought slammed through his mind. This must be how human queens wield power over their males, by giving and with-holding extreme pleasure. This is the kind of attention any warrior would kill to experience.

Her hand came up to caress his stomach, making his muscles tighten. "Why don't you lie back, and let me take care of you."

Backing off the sleeping platform, Larok shook his head. "I do not believe this is wise."

"What's wrong, babe?"

"I have no wish to give up so much of my personal power to you. Queens cannot be trusted."

His new queen moved forward to the edge of the sleeping platform and looked up at him. "Your damned queens have really messed with your heads when it comes to mating." Sliding off the platform and onto her knees before him, her hand came out to stroke him.

Something about seeing a queen kneeling before him stoked his lust, causing his mating scent to fill the air. Rising on her knees, she took him into her mouth again. If he'd though she wielded all the power before, this balanced things back out in his favor. His queen on her knees tending to his needs was a vision that would stick with him for many years to come. It was the type of fantasy warriors saw when they closed their eyes, pleasuring themselves, when they were alone and lonely.

The first time her overconfidence led her to take too much of him, his hand stroked and then fisted her glorious fire-colored strands. "Keep to the end, my precious. I like your tongue there best."

As she swirled her tongue around the tip in a never-ending dance of seduction, Larok found himself gently guiding her as he rocked himself against her tongue. Having a fistful of her beautiful strands made him feel like a god being served by his goddess. In that moment he began to understand her words about there being no hierarchy between males and females among her people. Humans generously gave to their mates and innocently accepted pleasure in return.

Pulling himself from her warm, wet mouth, he spilled his seed on her round globes. Seeing the blue-tinted clear liquid dripping down her pale flesh was satisfying in a way he never imagined possible. Somehow he thought feeling that way made him a very wicked warrior.

When her hands came up to rub his offering into her flesh, she didn't seem upset with him. Perhaps he wasn't wicked after all. Reaching all the way to her place on the floor, he lifted her in his arms. When their lips met, it was all teeth and tongues. Making the human kiss with her was something he would look forward to doing as often as possible.

"You please me more than I have words to say, my Hope."

"I enjoyed doing that for you. You smell and taste amazing, by the way."

Taking her hand, he sucked one finger into his mouth. "I taste fine, but your delicate female body tastes much better on my tongue." Her face pinked up more than usual. "Are you ready to sleep?" he asked.

"Only if you plan to wrap us up in your wings like last night. That was cozy."

Larok nodded. "This is a comfortable position for me as well. I love having your soft body so close to me while I slumber."

"You know something? Whatever is going on between the two of us is real, and it's got legs."

"I don't know what that means, my Hope."

"It means our relationship is going somewhere, instead of fizzling out. I honestly believe you are my one."

Knowing that queens always had a stable of breeders, Larok tried not to take her statement about him being her one too seriously. Truth be told, he was too happy with his lot in life for even the idea of sharing her to bother him this night.

Pulling back the thin bed covering, he held it open for her. Once she was on the platform, he joined her. She came easily into his arms and pressed her body against his. Larok carefully wrapped his wings around them and settled down to sleep. Contentment was a new feeling and one he much preferred over anxiety and fear. If they could make it safely to Naxis space, this could be a regular part of his life.

FINDING HERSELF STANDING IN FRONT OF A Draconian incubator, Hope peered through the viewing portal. The incubator was shaped like a large glass egg, and Larok's little one was lying on a small heating pad, gnawing at his fist, much like a human infant would. He had his father's coloring and big dark eyes. Excitement slammed through her body.

"This was your big secret?"

"Yes."

"Aww, he's the most adorable baby I've ever seen!"

Larok had been strangely quiet since they woke and had breakfast. He'd suggested that they visit the Draconian equivalent of a nursery. It honestly hadn't occurred to her to wonder if there were children on the ship. It now seemed like a serious oversight. If there was a queen and breeders, naturally there would be little ones.

Peering down at her, he asked, "You like the look of my little one?"

"Heck yea, he's freaking perfect. He even has little horns. When can we hold him?"

"He can come out today for a short interval. I will open the unit if you wish." After running his finger over the biometric lock, he pulled the front of the unit down. "It pains my soul that I was not able to be present for his shell-breaking ceremony. It happened while we were doing battle with the Zelerian ship. I am told the caregivers captured a vid of it for us to watch."

Seeing Larok with his son for the first time was sweet. The big warrior was so gentle and careful with the little newborn. Hope crowded close. "He's really cute, like his father. He's got your coloring, and those tiny wings are adorable."

"Our young always bear a strong resemblance to their sire, my queen."

"May I hold him?" Folding both of her hands together in front of her, she begged. "Please, just for a minute. I'll be really careful."

"I suppose. We take our young out for short intervals to hold them but he must go back in the chamber afterwards."

Once he had the little one in his arms, Larok seemed reluctant to let go of him. Hope couldn't help but tease him a little. "Don't be greedy with our son, babe. I'm dying to hold him." Trying to be funny only earned her a frown. Too excited to care, she carefully took the little one and laid him on her chest. "My goodness, he's so tiny and sweet. I hope he doesn't have to stay in the wall too much longer. That's no kind of life for baby."

"Our young are fragile for the first few days after they break out of their shell. When my little one has done his time, he'll be all the stronger for it."

Running one finger around his tiny jawline, she couldn't keep the smile off her face. "When he's ready, can we take him to our quarters?"

"Yes, if you wish. Normally, we have specially trained warriors who care for a warrior's hatchling."

"Why would we want some strange warrior caring for our child? The whole point of having a child is for us to enjoy raising him."

"This is true, I suppose. My father raised me and my brothers in his quarters once we were mature enough to look after ourselves."

"I never want to let this little guy go. He's too precious."

Chirping out a frustrated noise, Larok folded his arms over his chest. "Is this some kind of human joke at my expense?"

Her eyes jumped to his. "Okay, you've been acting all kinds of strange since we woke up. What gives?"

His eyes slid from hers. "Normally our queens will not tolerate the hatchling of another queen to live."

Shock rippled through her body. "Jesus, you think I'm going to harm your little one?"

"No! Well . . . yes, maybe."

"Decisive. I really like that in a mate." Her sarcasm didn't impress the now serious warrior one little bit.

"Draconian queens are strict about such things. I know human queens are different, but I do not know if this is a commonality with all females or only with our queens."

"You mean to say their symbionts don't want to worry with another queen's child. I'm guessing that's part of the crazy that makes them impossible to understand. If the critter inside makes all the decisions, why would it care who lives or dies?"

"You are correct, my queen. It makes little sense that they are so territorial in general and doubly so about tolerating another queen's young in their midst."

"Human women aren't like that at all. We tend to love babies, and we're not all that particular about where they come from. Since this one is yours and you're mine, I'm gonna get attached to him pretty darn quick."

"You still wish to bond to me, though I have bred with another queen?"

"Hell, yes! You are clearly worrying about a big bunch of things you don't need to give a second thought to. Once all this mess is behind us, we're going to settle down into one happy little family."

"I think he's getting chilled." Pulling open the top of her uniform, she tucked the baby into the top and pulled the fabric up over his trembling body. "There, that's better, isn't it, little guy?"

Larok's wings ruffled slightly. "You share your body warmth with my little one."

Glancing up at his concerned expression, she reminded him, "He's our little one, and I was just trying to keep him warm. Is having him against my skin forbidden?"

"Warriors often carry our young in such a way. Sometimes we nestle them in the top of our wing base, against our skin. It keeps them warm and safe."

"That's really sweet. What's his name?"

"Warriors do not normally name our young until their last reaping."

"What in the heck is a reaping?"

Looking away, he replied, "Our queens are particular about their offspring, as they see their young as a direct reflection on their breeding abilities. Queen Abraka normally reaps only the best at the time the eggs are layed. The ones deemed less than perfect are destroyed. She then comes back and reaps again just before the young are to break from their shell, and again when the little gems are deemed strong enough to remove from the incubator. Breeders learned long ago the futility of naming and getting attached to their young before the final reaping."

Hope's shocked eyes filled with tears, which began to spill down her face. She stammered, "No one is going to touch our little one, Larok. No one!"

He seemed almost as shocked as she was. "You are angry?"

Squeezing her eyes closed, she shook her head. "I can't talk about it, I just can't." Turning from him, she continued to nurture the innocent baby in her arms, as she worked to pull herself to together. That whole situation was ridiculous.

Damn the symbionts all to hell for forcing Draconian women to stand silently by, trapped in their own bodies, while the creatures killed off their young. Hope honestly couldn't imagine how horrific that must be for the poor women. A level of loathing and hatred Hope never thought herself capable of slid through her mind. After many long minutes she turned back to him.

"Children are the most vulnerable among us—they're so small and helpless. Therefore, we protect them. Anyone who would kill a newborn baby on purpose? I can't imagine it. I value children above all things. Such a fate will never befall our young."

His eyes slid away. "Since you are so fond of our young, shall I interview additional warriors for our family unit?"

Hope was about as close to totally bewildered as one woman could get. "You mean like in nannies or domestic help around our house?"

His eyes found her, his voice turned steely, and he practically spat the next words out of his mouth in an uncharacteristic fit of temper. "I mean as in additional warriors to breed for you."

"Oh babe, you are wearing me out today." It occurred to her that she'd just pissed the nice man off royally. Worst of all, she knew what had provoked his ire. She had made the survival of his child something that she had control over, like it was remotely her decision. That was all kinds of wrong. Her mind spun with a hundred things she wanted say in clarification of her stance on the subject, causing her to have a pounding headache. Sighing, she asked quietly. "Can we visit with our little one and talk this over later?"

He nodded and then sat with her, and they held the baby, marveling at how active he was. The tiny baby's curious eyes crawled over them as he kicked and tried to flap his wings. Hope rubbed his tummy and he made a soft chirping sound. He was too cute for words.

"My scion likes being cared for by you. Are you truly as thrilled as you seem to be, caring for another queen's young?"

"Absolutely! No woman would hold a child's parentage against him. On Earth, they have a one-child rule. Not that it matters, there are so many more women than men, someone like me would have never found a husband."

"Is that what prompted you to seek an alien mate?"

Nodding, she cuddled the little one against her neck. He made high-pitched chirping sounds as he rooted his face into the soft skin of her neck. His tiny wings flapped gently back and forth, much like a butterfly, though they were none too similar by design. "That was part of my reason for leaving Earth. It is also getting more difficult to survive on our world since the fall."

The tight anger slowly ebbed from his voice. "I cannot think what the fall might be."

"Pollution got so out of control, it poisoned our oceans and tipped our entire ecosystem off balance. Animals began dying out, and it took us a while to realize the pollution in the ocean created new and highly virulent germs. Our medical system had nothing to counteract the newly emerging diseases caused by the bacteria. We lost most of our animals, and our plant life slowly died off. It was all we could do to isolate most of the remaining population in gigantic bio domes. If not for that, we would have all succumbed to it."

Wrapping an arm protectively around her, Larok said, "We must make rescuing them a priority when we reach Naxis."

Smiling at him, she couldn't believe how sweet her new guy was. Her guy? Excitement zinged through her chest as she realized that she had an honest-to-goodness mate and a child. Doubt clouded her mind for a brief second, and she gave voice to her deepest worry. "Are you certain that you want to be with me?"

Looking down, he seemed to be concentrating. "I do not understand your question, my queen."

Waving one hand as she balanced the little one on her shoulder with the other, she explained. "Around these parts, warriors seem to roll with the punches. If a woman takes a liking to them, the warrior goes right on along with that. Don't you ever ask yourself what it is you want?"

"Warriors are afforded the privilege of choosing in your sector of space?"

Hope noticed several of the warriors in the large room made noises of disapproval. It was kind of funny, because she didn't think they'd been listening. "Well sure, warriors decide what jobs they want. When it comes to women, they have to want each other."

"You are suggesting that I have the choosing for more than just one night?"

Nodding, she smiled.

Larok reached in her uniform and pulled his little one out. After running his face lovingly over the newborn's face, he laid him carefully back into his incubator, quietly closing the lid. Turning to Hope, he took a deep breath. "You wished me to be your first breeder. That is why you selected me."

Nervously smoothing down her hair, Hope worried that maybe she'd gotten it wrong and he didn't really want her. Only last night, he seemed like he really did want her. She thought they'd come to a meeting of the minds.

"We don't consider our warriors breeders. I mean, you do breed, so I suppose it's expected that you will do that for me. It's just that we don't consider that the most important thing."

"I do not understand. What more can there be to like about a warrior?"

"Well for one thing, I think you're handsome and I like the way you move. It's kind of cool the way your muscles flex."

The poor warrior looked shocked. "You like the look of me more than my ability to breed?"

"Of course, I do. I also like your personality. On Earth, men were scarce on the ground, and since they could have any woman they wanted, it made them kind of arrogant. You're really sweet and strong and protective. You have a nice way about you."

Holding out his hand, he spoke. "You see me as different from other warriors? That is strange to me. One warrior is much like the next, with very little to distinguish us. Everything you have said about me is true of other warriors."

Taking his hand, she moved forward into the circle of his arms. Glancing down, she turned his words over in her mind. "I like that you automatically put your arms around me." His expression turned heated. She pressed her point. "You're also a good kisser. No other guy on this ship can love me the way you do." The gentle reminder about their intimate time the evening before seemed to drive her point home.

His eyes dropped down from her eyes to her lips. "I like making the human kiss with you, but I do not wish other warriors to see that."

"You don't want them thinking about kissing me, do you?"

"I know it is wrong to be selfish with a queen, but you are not like the queens we have known. You are small and warm and soft. The time will come when you select additional breeders. Until that time, I want to spend as much undivided time with you as possible."

Cupping his face with one hand, she whispered. "That sounds an awful lot like choosing me."

Cupping the other side of her face in his hand, he responded quietly. "If I were allowed the right of choosing, I would choose you above all the other queens we rescued. The moment I opened your escape pod, I felt something strange in my chest. A kind of want that I had not known until that moment."

"That's just the kind of sweetness I was talking about. Also, it's really cute that you think there is even a small chance of me developing my own little collection of warriors."

"You must, for our species to survive. I am not a true breeder. I will breed only one or two at a time."

"Not gonna happen. Remember we talked about how humans like small, manageable numbers of children. This is one area where more isn't necessarily better."

"I know you said that when you were distracted by my breeding scent. However, queens are rare, and..."

"Not where we're going. Remember, there were lots more women than men on Earth? There are hundreds of queens on your new home world, and more coming every day."

There were little noises of disbelief from the two remaining warriors on the other side of the room.

Throwing up her hands, Hope shot them an exasperate look. "I swear that I'm not making this shit up. There are millions of single women on Earth. Draconian ships just land outside their major cities to trade, and the women come pouring out of the bio domes asking for sanctuary on your new home world. There are more than enough women for every single warrior on this ship to have one. Hell, you can even afford to be selective."

One of the warriors spoke. "What of the queen who rules our new home world? Why would she tolerate thousands of women in her territory when she could have all the warriors for herself?"

Rolling her head back to stare at the ceiling, Hope took a deep breath. "The same reason I'm not battling it out with all the other women on this ship. Human women aren't like that. We usually bond one female to one male."

"You do not resent other women being in your territory?"

"I would hate to be stuck somewhere without other

women to talk to. Warriors are nice company, don't get me wrong. But sometimes a woman just needs some girl time."

Larok spoke. "Her words are true. The queens talk amongst themselves and cooperate, much like warriors. My Hope was very worried for the safety of her queen friends. They smiled and talked when we rescued them."

The other warrior spoke up. "How does Queen Cassandra win all the challenges to keep herself upon the throne?"

"I don't know what kind of challenge you're referring to specifically, but I seriously doubt many other women would want the responsibility of running an entire world. Do you have any idea how difficult that is? Most of us just want to settle down, have a home, and make a family. Sure, I want to contribute to our world in a meaningful way, but mostly I just want to enjoy my mate and raise our children." Hope looked from one to the other of the men. Clearly this was some kind of big news flash for them.

"Is that why we had to press you to be our queen when you first arrived?" Larok's voice was gentle as he stared down at her intently.

Hope could feel her face getting hot. "I've never been in charge of anything in my whole life. I didn't think I would be very good at it. Putting you all in danger because I'm incompetent seemed like a terrible way to thank you for saving my life. Thanks again, for that, by the way," she finished awkwardly.

"You have taken to leadership, just as we knew you would. Underestimating your own worth is a flaw that holds you back from becoming all that you are meant to be."

"I have to admit, being in charge isn't the nightmare I thought it was at first. Being surrounded by smart, competent men who aren't afraid to give advice is empowering. I might encourage you all to take your own good advice. Queen Cassandra's Draconian mate commands their military, and even sits on the throne when she isn't able to rule. Their world did not fall apart because a warrior wielded power."

"I fear it will take our warriors time to change our way of thinking on such matters."

HOPE

HOPE AND LAROK MADE ROUNDS ON THE SHIP. THEIR first stop was the bridge. Jeron was seated at the main operational panel, and he had warriors at the other five stations. He stood respectfully when they entered the room. "I believe you are here to be updated on our progress, Queen Hope. I have your daily report ready." Motioning towards the small office at the side, the older commander followed them into the room.

"That's real nice of you, commander. I was kind of curious about how things were coming along." Jeron sat behind a desk, and Hope and Larok occupied the two chairs in front of it. Hope chuckled—she'd traveled to a completely new sector of space, but this arrangement of offices seemed to be universal.

"We have translated the information in the Zelerian database relating to the worm hole generator and have successfully installed it on this ship. Our science team is running simulations to determine if it is functioning correctly."

"That sounds promising. Your team works fast."

"I assigned double teams to work continuous shifts, as we have no time to waste."

"Have we nailed down a timeline for the harvest yet?"

"We are planning to proceed with the harvest in twenty-seven hundred microns."

Hope did the math in her head. One minute was equal to three microns. That meant they would be ready to execute that mission in roughly fifteen hours. "Is everything else going well on the ship?"

"I believe all the queens are present and accounted for. Calen is engaged in a rather serious courting arrangement with your queen friend from the ship."

"I saw him with Ella last evening."

"As near as I can tell, about twenty percent of the queens have initiated courting with our warriors. I have been trying to rearrange scheduling to free them up to remain with their queens."

"That's really sweet, but I don't think the women will lose interest if the warriors need to work."

"That is good to know. I may have to assign them tasks during our upcoming missions. Some of them have special skill sets that we would be hard-pressed to do without."

"I think everyone on this ship would agree that our priority is to make it to free space. Nothing can be allowed to get in the way of that goal."

"Agreed. It is my understanding that you just visited the nursery."

Hope's face lit up. "I got to hold our little one. He's about the cutest baby I've ever seen. I can't believe he's perfect and he's ours."

"The caregivers reported that you were rather enthusiastic about discovering my scion had young."

"I have to admit he makes beautiful babies. I'm sure he gets that from his father."

The older man seemed to be smothering back a smile. "You are too kind, Queen Hope."

"I'm just really glad Larok and I hit it off so well. You have a fantastic family, and I'm proud to be joining it."

"It pleases me greatly to hear you say that. My scion is fortunate to have captured your notice."

"Well, that depends on how you look at it. In my eyes, I'm the lucky one."

"We are not used to such generous compliments from our females, Queen Hope. We thank you for your kind words. What is next on your agenda today?"

"I was kind of hoping to get a look at the wormhole generator. Then I'd like to check in on the other women. If it is permitted, I wouldn't mind finishing up our day by popping back into the nursery."

"All that sounds like a full day. Try to get some rest. I'm certain that being as curious as you are, you will wish to watch the harvest from the bridge."

"I suppose that would be for the best. Since I agreed to destroy a moon, I should be responsible enough to see that all goes well."

"Normally, our queens love to watch the explosions, as it validates they have the power to destroy worlds."

"I'm not wild about witnessing that kind of destruction. To me, it's more a matter of necessity than any kind of power trip."

"You are wise beyond your years, my queen. We are coming to trust your judgement in matters that relate to our survival and wellbeing."

"None of us want either of these missions to fail or

warriors to be unnecessarily harmed. I'm really glad that we can all agree about what's important."

"If anything changes, I will alert you immediately."

As they stood, Hope reached to grasp the commander's shoulder. "Thank you for all that you do. I don't know how we would get along without you."

"I live to serve, my queen."

"When this is all over, you should look for a loving age mate to keep you company on our new home world."

"I may consider that once the danger is past."

As they stepped onto the lift, Larok asked quietly. "Are you kind to our commander because of his contribution or because he is my sire?"

Turning to look at her anxious warrior, she responded, "Both. I honestly appreciate his leadership. He's an amazingly competent commander who keeps this ship operating and the crew on task. You are correct that I would still be fond of him if he held no position of importance, simply by virtue of the fact that he is family."

"That is a very concise answer."

"You know, humans believe that every person deserves to be treated with basic human dignity."

"I have noticed this in the way you interact with others. You are much like a warrior in that way."

Entering the engineering section, they made their way to the bay housing the wormhole generator. The room was filled with warriors she didn't recognize. They were moving around and some seemed to be making notes on data pads. One immediately moved forward to meet them.

"Do you wish a status report, my queen?"

"If you could just give me a short update, I'd like that. I don't want to waste too much of your time or interrupt the mission preparation."

"A queen could never be a disruption. I will give you the most important details. The unit has been installed. We had to remove it from the exterior of the Zelerian vessel and since fabricating a housing cradle on the exterior of our mother ship, we have bolted it to the floor of this loading bay. Our intention is to operate the unit with the bay door open. We've tested the functionality of the unit and it seems to be operating correctly. The Zelerian technology is somewhat similar to the device we were constructing for that purpose. I've had two teams working back-to-back to get both units operational. I believe the Zelerian device offers the best chance at generating a stable wormhole. However, I wish to use our own unit as a back-up, in case the Zelerian unit misfires."

"What would you say our chances of creating a stable wormhole that can actually transport us specifically to the Naxis?"

"We now fully understand the keying sequences. Therefore, if we are successful in opening a fully operational wormhole, we are assured to exiting into the correct sector of space."

"Congratulations on a job well done. The keying sequence was my biggest worry."

"Mine as well, Queen Hope. I believe we will be ready to make the jump in another rotation or two."

"I'll let you get back to it. If you need anything at all from me, please send for me right away.

The engineer dipped his head momentarily before replying. "I believe we are nearing completion of this task. I ask only that you bear with us a little longer, and then hold on tight as we jump to free space."

Hope's face lit up. "I can hardly wait. I hope you will

allow me to take your crew out for a small celebration when we reach your new home world."

"This would please us greatly, my queen."

As they exited the engineering section, Larok made a small sound of amazement. "You have the skills of a true queen when it comes to motivating our warriors."

"I wasn't trying to be motivational. Your engineering team is pretty awesome. I'd be an awful person if I didn't acknowledge their contribution. Where I come from, you don't get extra bonus points for treating people with the respect they deserve."

"I am coming to believe that you speak the truth about your kind."

"I wouldn't exactly go that far. Some humans can be selfish and self-serving, but most of us are pretty decent to one another."

Slipping his wing around her, Larok asked, "Would you like a proper tour of our ship. We have many interesting attractions."

"If any of it is half as attractive as you, it would definitely be worth a look."

HOPE

AFTER SPENDING THE DAY TOURING THE SHIP AND stopping in the dining unit for some dinner, they headed to the queen's chamber to check on the other women. The lift opened on the floor housing the queen's chamber, and they walked down a long corridor together. Hope asked, "What do you think our chances of getting to free space are? Do you think it is as good as they say?"

Larok paused briefly to consider her question. "I believe our chances are very good, if we do not attract the notice of any of the other queens."

"That was my thought as well. I don't know how we would hold up in a real battle and once they get close enough to scan for individual life signs, the other mother ships would swarm us."

Tugging her closer, he murmured, "Have no fear, my queen. We would fight to the last warrior to protect our queens."

The door to the queen's chamber opened and this time, many of the women were paired off with warriors rather than grouped in clusters with other females. Hope approached Stacy and Riya. "Where did Ella get off to?"

"They have some kind of mapping room with three dimensional holograms of this sector of space. Calen was nice enough to show it to her."

Larok interjected, "The cartography room had always held a great deal of fascination for my sibling. I'm not at all surprised that he's chosen to take her there."

Stacy shrugged. "She is an astronomer, so it sounds like a match made in heaven."

"Well, I'm happy for them. How has everything been going here?"

Riya responded quietly, "This is the nicest place I have ever been. The caretakers are really nice to us. They even fabricated me a new sari."

"It's a really nice one, as well."

Stacy smoothed down her form fitting gown. "Yea, these guys are making sure everything is all rosy for us. I've been worried about hooking up with a handsome warrior."

Hope sat down beside her friends. "What worries you?"

"I've been thinking the Taladar might want us back once we get back to Naxis. They paid good money for brides. I don't think they're just going to let us all wander off to the Draconian home world."

Hope wrinkled her nose. "I've been concerned about that as well."

Riya spoke up. "I do not think that will happen, my friends. I was worried about many things when I considered signing up for the intergalactic bridal registry. I worried that I might not turn out to be fertile or a genetic match for the alien race who purchased my contract. I worried that if I got hurt or sick, or if I died, they would press my family to refund the money the Taladar paid for me. I didn't want my parents to be forced into debt because of me."

"Jesus, I wasn't even smart enough to wonder things like that." Stacy's response took Hope by surprise.

"I have to admit that I didn't think of that either."

Riya smiled. "I researched it and discovered that we were all insured. If anything went wrong, the Taladar was reimbursed the bridal fees. I specifically asked if I would then owe the company who insured the transaction anything, and I was told in writing that I would not. Unless I miss my guess, that means we're all free and clear."

Hope gave her friend a quick hug. "You're definitely the brains of this operation, Riya."

Stacy squealed with delight. "This is the best news I've heard so far. I've got my eye on a nice little engineer."

"Go for it. Just remember that if we all want to get home safely, the guys need to focus on their jobs."

"Fair enough, I suppose. So, what's going on in the rest of the ship?"

"You're not going to believe this, but Larok has a son. He's the cutest baby I've ever set eyes on. He has little wings, just like his father. I'm totally head over heels for him, and I've only met him once."

"Do you have video or images?"

Shooting Larok a pleading look, she asked, "Do we have anything like that?"

"I created a direct video feed to his incubation unit. Would you like to see it?"

"Absolutely!"

Grabbing his com unit from his belt, he voice-prompted the feed to begin. Sure enough, a three-dimensional image popped up, showing him sleeping soundly on his cushion. His tiny wings fluttered a bit with each gentle snore.

"Sweet Jesus, you weren't even joking. He's perfect. I wonder how many of the guys here have little ones."

Gazing at the image, Hope responded absently mindedly. "I don't know how many exactly. There were at least a dozen babies in the nursery. I imagine there are some older kids running around somewhere on this ship as well. The old queen was probably breeding right up until the end."

Stacy asked excitedly, "Can we visit your little one?"

Hope's head snapped up. "Not yet. He's too small. I don't want everyone breathing on him."

Stacy tossed her a lopsided smile. "Afraid he might catch some human cooties, or halitosis perhaps?"

Trying not to look as embarrassed as she felt, Hope chose her words more carefully. "Draconians haven't been around humans before, so we're taking extra precautions with him. He's not even old enough to be out of the incubator for more than a few minutes. The little guy just isn't ready for visitors."

Riya suggested diplomatically. "Perhaps when he is ready for visitors, we can hold a welcoming party for him. We will all be careful not to crowd him."

Reaching out to touch Riya's hand, Hope smiled. "That would be fantastic. Thanks for understanding."

Stacy quipped, "Who's understanding? I still want to hug him all up and give him big sloppy kisses."

Hope laughed merrily. "You are on the verge of getting yourself disinvited to the welcoming party altogether."

Drawing her face into a pretend pout, Stacy responded, "You're a real party pooper. I hope you know that."

"If I had to guess, I'd say you were a stand-up comedian on Earth."

"Wrong again."

"I've been trying to guess your occupation since we met. Come on, toss me a clue already."

Tapping her nails on her teeth, Stacy thought it over. "I'm fascinated by babies for a reason."

"You were a daycare provider."

"Not even close."

"I would guess pediatrician, but none of them ever would sign up for the bride's registry because they have good lives on Earth."

Tilting her head to one side, her friend stared at her. "All except the ones whose parents are forcing them into marriage with pompous asshats who think women should bow down and let them do whatever they want."

"Are you serious?"

"I signed up for the bride's registry, hoping for a better husband. It looks like I hit the hot-husband jackpot."

"You seem too irreverent to be a physician."

"Stereotyping went out of style decades ago, my friend."

"Well, since you're a physician, maybe you could check our little one over. I'm sure he's fine, but a well-baby visit never hurts, right?"

Smiling, Stacy shrugged. "I probably should have started the conversation with a little bragging instead of begging."

Riya leaned forward. "Do you think I might be able to come as well, if I promise to just watch from across the room?"

Standing, Larok nodded. "That will be fine, but only the two of you. We should leave here before someone else overhears your conversation and wishes to join us."

A few minutes later, they were standing in the nursery, staring at Larok's newborn. Stacy's voice sounded off. "Wow, video images do not do him justice. Seeing him in person is amazing. You can see the tiny little blood vessels running under his skin. No wonder they are so careful with them for the first few days. I'll bet his skin is still developing. Those wings look pretty fragile as well."

Riya pressed her hand against the glass. "He has a beautiful spirit. I can tell these things." Wandering off, she began looking at each baby in turn. One of the nursery attendants walked over to her.

Larok walked off to speak to another of the attendants.

"I still can't believe you're a pediatrician."

"Yep, I was real nerd growing up. Somehow, I didn't come into my own until my parents began pressuring me to get married. That's what made the lion inside roar to life."

"I'll bet it did. You know that most of us are indigent, don't you?"

"Well, that doesn't quite carry the negative connotation it once did. Since the fall, about eighty percent of our population is destitute. As you can see, I don't care much about money and status. I just want to find a little happiness."

"I'm right there with you on that one, sister."

Several of the nursery attendants approached them. An older one spoke. "My name is Amok, and someone told me you are a healer on your home world, Queen Stacy."

"I'm a healer specifically for infants. On Earth, healers are broken into different specialties. I'm actually a pediatric neurosurgeon. I treat anything related to the brain, spinal cord, and nervous system."

"That's quite fascinating. You wish to examine Larok's newly hatched scion?"

"I'd love to have a look at him. Draconian physiology interests me, particularly the biology of the wing area that runs along the spinal cord. Humans don't have that particular piece of anatomy."

"We have a small exam room where we treat minor illnesses and injuries. Our young are quite hardy and resilient, so mostly the room is used to track their growth and progress through early developmental stages. If you would like, I will walk you through a typical examination performed at this particular stage of development. Since you are a healer, you are welcome to visit anytime. We will be happy to share information with you."

"That's a very generous offer. Perhaps I could share information about human physiology. Since you've never encountered humans before, you must have a ton of questions."

Smiling faintly, Amok replied, "That was actually going to be my next suggestion." The small group wandered off to show Stacy the exam room.

Hope hopped up onto her toes and kissed Larok's jaw. It was pretty much all she could reach without him bending down. His arms came up around her, and he dipped his head to capture her lips. He must have forgotten all about not kissing her in front of other warriors. Pulling back, he gazed down at her. "You make me proud to be your protector."

"Does that mean I get to hold our baby?"

Opening the glass front of the unit, he lifted out the sleeping infant and placed him in her arms. "I find it impossible to deny you any request, Hope."

Grinning like a mad fool that he'd used her name without some corny title attached to it, she gave him a hug with one arm. "I'm seriously falling in love with you. I hope you know that."

Laughing, he pulled her closer, with the little one between them. "The translation program is selecting the word taneka for the word love, but I am not your child."

"Taneka is Draconian for love?"

"It is the bond between a warrior and his young. I taneka my little one as well as my father and brothers."

"We use the word love for people we have particularly strong affection for. Don't you have a word that means taneka between a warrior and his queen?"

His eyes grew perfectly round. When he spoke it came out a reverent whisper. "Takadon. In olden times, when our queens held a warrior in high esteem, he became her takadon. It is the highest privilege that can be bestowed upon a male. It meant that they were joined together as one and inseparable. Wherever she went, he followed."

Hope replied confidently, "You're definitely my takadon."

His wings came out and wrapped around her and the baby. Hope turned slightly and rested the side of her head on his chest, as she looked down into the face of her tiny sleeping son. "This feels like the most perfect moment of my entire life."

Tucking her head under his chin, Larok whispered, "This is all a warrior needs to find true happiness. Under my wings you will always find love, peace and safety."

LAROK

WALKING BACK TO THEIR TINY NEST FELT DIFFERENT tonight. Rubbing his chest with one fist, Larok tried to understand how he felt about what had just transpired between the two of them. Not only had he been selected for breeding, but he had been named her takadon. That would normally make him first among her males. That was an honor beyond his wildest aspirations, but she had also made it clear that he was to be her one and only male. He still couldn't get his head around having a queen for all his own. It seemed wasteful somehow.

The more he thought about the way she described their life together on their new home world, the more desperately he wanted it. She said she wanted a home. He'd seen homes when they were planetside. They were spacious enclosures high in the trees. Since all beings had wings, there was no need for lifts or anything of that nature. Clearly their home would either need to be closer to the ground, or he would need to ferry her up and down.

Pride surged in his chest that she had so willingly accepted his scion. Seeing her tenderly caring for him made his chest hurt. The reality set in that she had extended her queen protection to his little one. He doubted any of the other queens would be so generous. No, his queen was generous beyond measure.

"You look so serious. What's up, handsome?"

"I have learned many new things in a very short period of time. I was not bred for intelligence, but to be a warrior. Forgive me Hope, I am working hard to process all that is happening."

"You're smarter than I am about most things."

"I wish to give you my sincere gratitude for naming me your takadon. It is a great honor, and one no Draconian male has enjoyed in centuries."

"Wow, I didn't know it was such a big deal. Do you think we need to slow down?"

"I don't know how that will help us in this situation, because when it comes to you I only ever want more. To have a queen, a child, and a new home world—with true freedom—are almost more than I can imagine."

"What did you always think your life would be like?"

Waving his hand over the scanning plate leading to their room, he sucked in a deep breath. "I assumed my life would be short and fairly pointless. When I was accidentally subjected to Queen Abraka's pheromones and produced a little hatchling, it totally reoriented my thinking. Since none of my sire's scions have been selected as breeders, we were looking at our clade dying out. My task seemed fairly straightforward, work with my family to protect my hatchling and see that our clade survived."

"What do you mean by your clade? You use the word almost like species."

Larok began undressing his queen, to ready her for cleansing. "Each of us is descended from a specific set of

Draconian genetic code, paired with humanoid genetic matter. This pairing is why we no longer have fire in our blood."

"On Earth there are myths about men who shift into dragon form."

Snorting a laugh, he couldn't seem to stop chuckling. "Creatures do not simply transmute into other creatures. The whole idea behind your myth defies the laws of nature."

Grinning like a mad fool, Hope pinched him playfully on the hip. "Make fun of me, will ya? Well, I won't stand for it."

Still smiling, he continued speaking. "Forgive me, my breathtakingly beautiful queen. Since you seem curious I will tell you that there are tens of thousands of different base codes that determine our combination of exact skin markings, the shape of our wings and such. Though our physical attributes are dominant and pass along almost undiluted, our gifts are sometimes diminished."

"I did notice you are all subtly different. What do you mean by gifts?" She tried not to seem as happy as she was that he was peeling her out of her uniform.

"We all have different gifts. Some can scent with their horns. In others the horns are connected to their auditory physiology in such a way that it enhances their hearing. Others regenerate more quickly, run or fly faster. Others were gifted breeders and can produce many young in a single breeding cycle. Those with the gift of breeding are used almost exclusively by our queens for that purpose. They can produce up to two times two hands of young in a single cycle."

"I never heard anything about that." Stepping into the mister as he gestured, Hope turned to watch him undress.

Since he was her takadon, she enjoyed the sight of his naked body. Her eyes drifted from his face down to his chest and paused to admire his manhood, before moving down to his legs and feet. "You have nice feet." Shaking her head slightly she brought her head back up to look him in the eyes. "What is the gift of your line?"

Moving closer, he acknowledged quietly. "As I said before, I am a poor choice in breeders, for I can only produce hatchlings one or two at a time. I cycle three or four times a year. It is one reason our line is dying out."

"That sounds perfect to me." They stepped into the cleansing unit. "We've already talked about this a couple of times and I'm not about to change my mind. Besides, I can make babies too. You know that, right?"

Rubbing cleansing foam onto her body, Larok snorted a laugh. "Queens do not breed. They consider that task to be beneath the dignity of a queen. It rarely happens for our queens, and they are usually furious when it does."

"Yeah, those symbionts must not like sharing space inside the queen's body. It probably gets pretty cramped in there."

A trill of surprise escaped his throat before he could stop it. "By the gods you are right, Hope. I never would have thought about that, but if it is as you say, that the parasite attaches to the queen and spreads, that may very well be the reason. My soul aches to think our queens are being used in such a way."

His new queen moved closer and wrapped her arms around him, as best she could with all his bulk. "I'm really sorry that happened to your people. I wish there was something we could do to help them."

Larok's head came up hard and fast. "Never think such a thing. There are too many to fight and they are nothing like Earth females. You wouldn't stand a chance in a challenge match." Pulling her close, he tried to push away the thought of her getting mangled in combat.

Her soft hands began moving over his body, rubbing in the cleansing foam. She traced the delicate patterns on his skin with one finger, clearly delighting in one of the few subtle differences that distinguished him from other males. It was sufficiently distracting enough for him to forget everything else. All the dangers of their situation seemed far removed from this moment in time.

She murmured approvingly, "You have lots of muscles."

Trying not to seem proud, he made light of her comment. "I have less than most, more than some."

"You told me all about the qualities lines have, but not what unique offerings your line possesses."

"I do not know that you would believe me."

"Try me, handsome."

Taking a deep breath, he disclosed his families' unique quality. The one they normally kept secret, since others would surely revile them for possessing such a gift. "We are feelers, in that we are drawn to the truth of a matter before we have information to fully support it as fact. I didn't have any reason to think your escape pod held a queen until I got within scanning distance. Yet, I was drawn inexplicably to seek it out. I don't think I could have stopped myself if I wanted to, even though I worried that it contained a bomb or biological contagion."

"Maybe I am a biological contaminant. The ancients of Earth believed in love spells." Noticing his confused expression, she laughed. "Love spells are words, prayers or incantations that make person fall hopelessly in love with another person."

"That you jest with me is sweet. I love hearing about

your people." Dropping a kiss on her lips, he continued. "The very moment I opened the pod, I had the strongest feeling that you were meant to be my queen. The idea of being chosen by a queen, much less a soft, beautiful queen like yourself, above true breeders was so fantastically improbable that I honestly thought maybe my gift was leading me astray."

"Wow, you really can sense things."

"Considering my line has no natural advantages to assist a warrior, save this, I would have to say yes. Many stronger lines have died out, but mine remains."

"Your father and brother have it as well?"

"Yes. When we are all touching, the feeling is concentrated. I know this will not make sense, but I can be nothing but honest with you, Hope. When we concentrate our strength, my sire can sense what is going on over great distances and sometimes accurately predict a future event. That is how we knew our brethren were free in your sector. He saw it in his mind's eye and then we verified it by networking the warriors on other ships. We learned that a first wave had been sent by the elder warriors in hopes of finding a place where queens did not control every aspect of our lives."

"Well, they sure found it. Is your entire family on board this ship?"

"Regrettably not, I have three siblings on the ship belonging to Queen Lakara. They were separated from us almost a full lunar ago."

"Is there any way to get them back?"

"Not that I or my family can sense. It is frustrating to be separated. It feels like something important is missing from my life."

Running her hands down to his rod, she lathered him

up. "We'll have to keep thinking on how to best address that problem. I will not leave them behind. Perhaps there is a way to trade for them."

"I would risk my own life a thousand times to see them safely to our ship." Sucking in a sharp breath, Larok murmured, "Your touch is very arousing. Better than anything I have known."

"Do you know that when our males are frustrated about things they have no control over, we sometimes soothe them with sex."

Letting out a shocked trill, his response was immediate. "In that case, many things frustrate me. Shall I list them all?" His queen laughed at his jest and for a moment, Larok felt better. "Your happy sound is pleasing to my ears."

"You are almost ready to spill, I can feel it."

"Though I am not a breeder, I am still a male and none would fail to be aroused by one such as you, my queen."

"You're allowed to touch as well, you know that right?"

"I thought that was a privilege extended only for one night."

"Nope, last night was our warm up. Tonight, we go all the way."

Running his hand down grip the base of his member, Larok stroked himself a couple of times. He brazenly ran his hands over his small soft queen, squeezing her soft mounds gently. Toying with her soft peaks, he lifted her with both wings to taste her water slickened skin.

Whatever he thought mating was from standing guard for his former queen during a mating cycle, being with his human queen was nothing very similar. Rather than drawing blood with her claws, she scraped them gently over his skin, causing arousal rather than pain. Sliding her down his body, he allowed her feet to touch the floor.

When she ran her hand over his rod again, Larok felt a jolt of arousal so strong it took him by surprise. His senses were sounding off on an infinite loop in his head, telling him to pleasure his queen. No, it was a subtly different message. He wanted to claim her as his own, protect her and shelter her under his wing for all times. Warriors normally didn't feel this way about their queens. The fact that she's forsworn all other males in favor of being only with him, provoked a level of possessiveness he didn't think himself capable of before this moment.

Everything about this moment seemed amplified and more intense compared to the night before. Larok suspected it was because he was now her takadon and tonight was their first true mating. Adding to the heady mix was the scent of her pheromones. She was at the peak of her fertility cycle. It was clearly noticeable from several steps away. Getting out of the cleansing unit, he held out one hand.

Tossing him a lopsided smile, she teased, "Bath time's over, is it? That didn't last long."

"My unique gift is telling me it's is time to pleasure you." Smiling, he continued, "I find myself quite eager to enjoy all the delights that have been thus far forbidden to me by our own queens with the one I love."

Throwing back her head, she laughed. "I think you're just making this up as you go."

Coming to an abrupt halt, he looked down into her smiling face. "You doubt that my gift rings true?"

Smiling up at him, she replied happily. "Heck no, I plan to enjoy your gift for many years to come. You know, humans believe in something very similar to what you're describing. We call it intuition and it is reputed to be stronger in females than males."

Something loosened in chest at her open acceptance of

the trait that had enabled his line to survive for hundreds of solar revolutions, while other stronger lines had faded from existence.

He picked her up and began walking again, so eager to mate that he'd completely forgotten about the drying cycle. "A warrior must have skill in addition to gifts in order to please his queen."

Reaching her hand up to cup his face, she replied. "I think you've more than got that covered, babe."

Dropping her unceremoniously onto the sleeping platform he informed her solemnly. "I will make the revidian again tonight just the same, so you might know me for the honorable warrior that I am."

Sitting up, she asked, "What the heck is that?"

Leaning over the bed Larok pressed two fingers again between her thighs. "It is when I put my mouth here, for your pleasure. I believe you enjoyed the revidian very much when I last performed it on you."

Scooting to the side of the platform, she reached for his thick member, using it to playfully tug him forward. Breathless anticipation slammed through his chest at the thought of her soft tongue pleasuring him again. She seemed pleased to touch him again. Glancing up she murmured, "Human women love to revidiawhatever their men. We do it every chance we get."

Staring down, Larok watched her lean forward and put her mouth on his rod. His mating scent was back again with a vengeance. Running her hands down his rod, the eager little queen pleasured him with abandon. It was all too easy to quickly get drawn to the edge of his control by her warm mouth.

Pulling back, he choked out, "You must stop. I will not

be satisfied spilling anywhere except inside my queen this night." Easing her back, he positioned her for the revidian.

"The warriors talk about many things, but none more than the revidian. Not being seen as a potential breeder, I had never been trained on exact positioning. Last night in my eagerness, I didn't realize how easily the technique would be to figure out."

"Well, you were perfect."

Separating her delicate folds the sight before him was even lovelier than he remembered. Unable to contain his excitement, he tasted her with long firm strokes. As he got lost in exploring her body, he had no idea how she compared to a Draconian queen, nor did he care.

He could tell by her response that his precious queen loved the revidian almost as much as he did. The sounds coming out of her mouth were something only a queen could make and shoved his need to new heights. When his queen came apart under this tongue, he forced himself to stop so she could catch her breath.

She was beautiful, particularly after being pleasured. The strands growing from her head were fanned out across the pale bedding reminding him of a decorative work of art. Larok thought it must feel strange to have so many strands growing out one's skin. Speaking of skin Hope's body was now blushing the same color as her face did sometimes. It was quiet appealing.

"You look very pleased with yourself."

"Every warrior wishes to pleasure his queen, even low status ones like me. It is everything the breeders bragged it up to be and necessary to prepare you for what is to come."

"I've been fantasizing about that a lot over the last couple of days."

"Mating is said to be a true joy when the queen is in her fertile phase."

"My what? Never mind, I know what you mean. I must be ovulating."

Larok tried to keep some semblance of control, when truth be told, he wanted to climb on top and do unspeakable things to her naked body.

"What position are you thinking about?"

"There is only one. The queen is always on top of her warrior. That is the natural order of things."

"We'll try out a few."

"You have mated before?"

Nodding, she scooted back to make room for him. "This ain't my first rodeo, cowboy."

"I do not know what that means."

"Sit back. It means we are going for reverse cowgirl first. Don't worry. Unless I miss my guess, you will like it."

Leaning back on his hands, he watched his queen ease down onto his rod. "I do not think you are sized correctly for a warrior."

"Somehow, I thought you were going to say that. No worries. I got this."

She was correct. The wetness of her body allowed her to slowly absorb most of his endowment. "Wow, you feel really nice."

Between the pleasure of feeling her tight body wrapped around his and her sweet compliments, Larok could hardly think of a reply.

Turning to look over her shoulder, she asked, "Are you ready, babe?"

Nodding, he pulled himself together enough to answer. "Always, my queen."

When she moved, Larok knew why it was that breeders

were so protective of their queens. Breeding made life worth living. Though he knew from the first moment he'd seen her in the life pod that he would give his life for hers, now he felt it in his soul.

Reaching one hand around to cup her breast, he teased her soft peaks, making her bounce ever more enthusiastically on his rod. This particular cause and effect intrigued him, for he wasn't used to eliciting such a desirable response from a queen. Sliding his other hand around, he slid his fingers through her tender folds, searching for the tiny nub that drove her wild when he teased it with his tongue. Larok was thrilled to discover it provoked a similar reaction when he was inside her luscious body.

HOPE

WHEN HOPE WOKE UP, SHE WAS DRAPED OVER HER handsome warrior. Last night had totally blown her mind. All she had to do was give a little instruction paired with a demonstration or two, and Larok was the kind of guy who could really run with it. They'd done the reverse cowgirl, cowgirl, and missionary. Being on their knees with him behind had been super-hot, but having him pound her into the wall was the one she'd never forget. Larok seemed awed by the missionary, probably because warriors didn't mount queens in his neck of the woods.

If she ever felt like they hadn't known each other long enough to be sure about being together, she'd think of last night. They'd both had more pleasure than either of them had hoped to enjoy in a lifetime in one short night. Larok was the one—she could feel it in her bones. This was worlds better than being assigned a bride by the Taladar once they got to their home world. At least she knew and really liked Larok. It was hard to resist having sex with a hot warrior when she'd spent her entire adult life being deprived of inti-macy. Maybe they were moving too fast. The bottom line was that it really didn't matter so much to Hope, because sometimes in life, you just have to roll the dice. This truly felt right in almost every way.

Shifting into a more comfortable position, she caressed his muscular chest, tracing the fanciful barely noticeable patterns on his skin. Everything about him far surpassed every expectation she had about being with a man. Whoever thought she'd end up with a gorgeous guy, a new home world that was reputed to be a virtual paradise, and a newborn son? This was truly a dream come true in her eyes.

Tamen's voice came from nearby. "Would you like a morning drink, Queen Hope?"

Snatching her covering up over them both she sputtered, "Tamen, what are you doing here? You shouldn't be here."

Larok sat up, stretching his arms. "He is your keeper. The one who helps you bathe and polishes your claws. You are lucky to have one day off from his attentions."

Swallowing hard, Hope looked around the room to see two warriors she didn't know standing against the far wall. The room was simply too small to accommodate so many people. "What in the hell is going on here?"

"Do not be alarmed, my queen. All is as it should be."

"I don't like people besides you seeing my naked bottom."

Smiling indulgently, Larok replied, "You have a very nice bottom. Therefore you have nothing to be ashamed of, my Hope."

When she looked at her handsome warrior, she could tell he wasn't fully awake yet. His horns were still drooping crazily, one leaning forward and the other back. Trying to keep her indignant tone in place, she couldn't help but notice that he looked like he'd been fucked senseless. Why did that make her so flipping happy?

Clearing her throat, she stated firmly. "I thought we gave them the slip. We're here for some intimate time together, remember?"

"I am not supposed to stand in the way of your assistants ...um...assisting you." God, he was totally out of it. Using the same word twice in a row was a dead giveaway.

"You are my takadon. Make them go away." The sternness in her voice gave way to one of admiration as she scooted towards him. Leaning over, she gave the sleepy man a kiss on the cheek and nuzzled her face against his because let's face it, he was adorable in the morning.

Surprised chirps sounded off from the other males, and Tamen's awestruck voice sounded off. "Your takadon? Larok is your forever mate?"

"I've been saying that repeatedly, only no one's been listening."

Tamen stated worriedly, "I do not think the elders will approve of your being left to your own devices by your assistant. It is not right to do that to our queen."

The rose tint was wearing off her morning pretty damn fast. Tossing the covering aside, she began to climb out of bed. "You know what? I don't even care if you see everything God gave me. I can't sit around here and argue all day. We have brothers to rescue and a moon to destroy."

Larok bolted upright, jumped out of bed, and followed her into the cleansing room. "We have what to rescue?"

Stepping into the mister, she began rubbing cleansing foam over her body. "Your brothers, tell me more about the ship that they've been assigned to."

Stepping into cleansing unit, he also began washing his body. "They serve a newly made queen. When a new queen is fitted with her first ship, each mother ship contributes males to make a full complement of warriors for her crew."

Quickly washing her hair she ducked under the water to rinse it. Larok stood gaping at her. She hit the button on the drying unit, and the mister stopped as warm jets of air began shooting out. Together they finger-combed her hair. Hope was beginning to rely upon the small rituals they were creating. It gave her some measure of stability in an otherwise unpredictable situation. Plus, she liked the way his fingers felt running through her hair.

Strolling stark naked back into the sleeping room, she pulled on her fresh underthings and snatched up the crisp new custom-made uniform that Tamen had fabricated for her. It was trimmed in red and had more fancy trim around the sleeves and high neck. It was truly clothing fit for a queen. An exact replica of her uniform had been created for Larok.

Hope said, "We need to talk to the elders. See if they can meet with us after breakfast."

Larok looked up from examining his new uniform. "I do not recognize this design. Why has our uniform changed?"

Tamen began busying himself pulling the bedding from the sleeping platform. "You will need to discuss that with your sire and the elder council."

Hope's exasperated voice sounded off. "We have more important things to worry about, like getting your brothers back on this ship before we jump to the Naxis."

"I will call the elder council together, my queen. They are not going to wish to engage in combat with the young queen over three warriors of little import. Their priority is seeing to the harvest and then using the wormhole generator to escape."

"We can argue about that later. Right now, I'm starving. Let's get something to eat and meet up with the elders." Placing a reassuring hand on Tamen's arm, she winked at him. "I'm sorry for being such a grouch. You're right, I'm gonna need some nail polishing real soon. Hang in there. You're not out of a job quite yet."

His annoyed expression smoothed out. "All will be as you wish, my queen. I will offer my services to the other queens for today."

"That's a great idea." Stopping long enough for Tamen to pull a large comb through her hair, she sipped the hydration pouch he shoved into her hands. "Yum, it tastes like coconut. I'm sure the other women would love to have your company for the day. Who knows, you might find yourself a queen from among the multitude of women."

Smiling at her, his horns perked up in a display of interest. "Perhaps you are right. We will have to see if any warm to me. Meanwhile, if you have need of me do not hesitate to message me."

"Will do. Have a nice day and good luck luring a queen." Stopping at the door, Hope turned to Tamen. "Do you have children?" With his past of serving the elder queen so closely, something made her think he did.

He nodded warily. "I have three who are less than a solar old. They are just now flying under the power of their own wings."

"I'll bet they're adorable. Most human women absolutely love little ones. You might want to introduce yours around. You'll probably end up having your choice among several queens if they know they're getting little ones in the bargain."

"You jest!"

"Let's just say meeting Larok's little one only made me like him more."

Tamen's head dipped slightly. "Thank you for that bit of information, my generous queen."

"You're more than welcome, my friend. Good luck queen hunting."

Several shocked gasps could be heard as she walked away. As they walked to the dining room, Hope grabbed Larok's hand. "I had a dream last night."

"A pleasant one, I hope."

"No, it was more of a nightmare. I dreamed that I went to the medical bay and somehow, the stasis field around Queen Abraka failed. Her symbiont disengaged from her body and ran me down. I remember this excruciating pain in my side as it penetrated my skin."

Wrapping an arm around her, her protective warrior pulled her close. "Our stasis fields never fail. They are reliable. I sense no problems in that area."

Entering the dining hall, Hope grabbed a plate and began tossing food onto it. "I was thinking. What about if we disengaged the stasis field intentionally? If the parasite knows it's losing its host, wouldn't it try to move to another one?"

"I suspect that if they took chances like that, we would have discovered their deception long ago."

"If they're as smart as I think, they probably only do things like that when they're certain of success. Maybe if I'm alone in the room and pretend to be vulnerable, it might risk exposure by trying to get to me."

Sitting down at one of the tables, Hope looked at him, pleading with her eyes for him to agree. Larok couldn't find it in his soul to approve such a foolhardy plan. "You wouldn't be pretending to be vulnerable. You would be in great danger if your hunch is correct."

"I think it's worth the risk."

"Who would lead us if you were killed?"

"Jesus, you guys don't need me. You're doing wonderful all on your own. On top of that, you have a hundred other women here who can pretend to be queen."

His voice dropped a level. "I do not wish to continue without you, my Hope."

Popping a bite of food in her mouth, she sighed. "Then figure out a way for us to do this safely. You are a warrior, after all."

Thinking it over as he ate, Larok mused out loud. "We can't set a second level-one stasis field within close proximity to another. It interferes with the functionality of each unit. If not for that, I would suggest we arrange for Abraka's stasis field to fail and leave another field open between you and her. I wouldn't take a chance on either unit failing."

"How about positioning weapons around the room and killing the symbiont once it leaves Abraka's body?"

"I might be able to come up with some ideas that could save your skin if the symbiont attacks."

LAROK

Elder Jeron swallowed thickly. "Since you asked me for my opinion, my answer is no and no. Both of your suggestions are fraught with danger."

Elder Thermon murmured his agreement. "What you suggest is very dangerous. We discovered the public service bulletin from Queen Cassandra. It was very enlightening and worrisome. It seems that the symbionts are small water-borne creatures when they first enter the body, and then they grow. There's no telling how large they get or how they graft themselves to the interior bone structure or organs. If a full-grown parasite infected you, it would most likely be life threatening. Our queen is much larger than you. If the symbiont has matured inside our elder queen, it may not even fit inside your body without doing substantial damage."

Leaning over the table to stare them down, his queen refused to take no for an answer. "This is an opportunity to kill two birds with one stone. We want to save the elder queen if we can. To do that, we need to get the symbiont to abandon her. They can be killed. Without a host, they are as vulnerable as you or me. That's what I think of your first no."

Jeron shook his head. "Regarding your second suggestion of the day, drawing the notice of the young queen is perilous. Thinking you can trick her into trading my three siblings back to us is pure folly. Newly minted queens routinely choose to battle for resources rather than barter. They are extremely unpredictable and aggressive."

"Sure they are. Those young girls are engaged in the fight of their lives, with the symbionts trying to control them. All I know is, if we can free Abraka, she can help us lure the young queen. If the young queen thinks Abraka is weak, she may be ambitious enough to want to try to best her in combat to acquire this mother ship. You have to admit it would be a huge upgrade compared to that little training ship she's currently calling home. If this young Queen Lakara senses opportunity, she'll jump at the chance to better herself. The symbionts are supposedly easier to pry from the younger queens because they haven't grown and wrapped themselves around their internal organs."

Elder Thermon's shocked voice sounded off. "You wish to save a Draconian queen?"

"I want to save two if we can, the elder queen Abraka and the young queen. In the interest of full disclosure, I mostly want Larok's brothers off that ship. I'm not leaving my takadon's brothers behind under any circumstances, so we better figure out a way to make it happen."

Hope gave them a moment for her words to sink in. Their shocked expressions communicated how bizarre they thought it was to try to wrest three warriors back from a Draconian queen.

After giving them a minute, she pressed her point again. "Once we have the young queen, we put her in stasis, destroy the moon, and send every shuttle on the harvest. While they are harvesting, we put the wormhole generator through its final tests to make sure it's stable, after that we create a wormhole and exit into the Naxis. With any luck we'll be gone before the rest of queens suspect what's going on."

"How do you propose getting Queen Lakara off the training ship?"

"Larok and I will board with a small party of warriors and set a trap in the loading bay. When she comes to challenge me, we spring the trap. Hopefully Abraka will be alive and recovering. Jeron will be in charge of this vessel. You'll use a wormhole generator to open a portal. Then we fly both ships through the portal, making sure it closes behind us."

"What if another ship makes it through before the wormhole closes."

Turning to look at elder Thermon, Hope replied, "We'll cross that bridge when we get to it. If we keep thinking up hypotheticals and solving them all day, we're not going to get anything done. This is a solid plan. I say we work the plan."

Elder Thermon mused out loud. "We could save the young queen, perhaps Queen Abraka if she is strong enough, harvest a vast supply of resources and make our escape. If we are careful, we might be able to make it look like our ships got sucked into an anomaly, and the other queens will none be the wiser. It's a good plan, if we can pull it off."

Jeron nodded. "I would risk much to see my family reunited. So be it, Queen Hope. We will flesh out your plan and see what might be the best way to proceed."

"I say we try to save Abraka first. She might give us some insight into how to handle the rest."

Larok spoke up for the first time during their conference. "I may have a solution for protecting my queen when she lures Abraka's symbiont. I believe the creature is only as capable as its host. We know that due to her advanced age, Queen Abraka has lost much of her vision and hearing. The stasis unit will prohibit her from being aware of what is going on around her. Once the stasis unit is disengaged, I propose that we use the maintenance robots housed in the ceiling of the medical bay to destroy the symbiont as it moves across the room to my queen. I wish to be at the controls, because the controller will only have one shot to stop the symbiont. No one is more motivated to keep a queen alive than her own takadon."

His sire stood. "Agreed. How much time to do you need to prepare the maintenance unit?"

"I can have it done in one hand times three."

"That is forty-five microns. I will take Queen Hope to be fitted with armor. In the event that it gets to her, I wish there to be a last layer of defense. It will give us a few precious microns to get to her if things go bad."

Everyone went their separate ways, and Larok headed to the maintenance unit. Calling the maintenance unit from the medical bay, he pulled the two large arms down and began working on the unit. Every area had a maintenance bot. They were basically two large arms that folded down from the ceiling to work on anything that needed fixing. Maintenance techs usually performed more difficult tasks in person, but simple tasks were performed remotely. It kept techs from running all over the ship constantly.

Removing the multi-tool from one hand, he attached a laser pistol and adapted a triggering mechanism.

Concerned that it might somehow fail, he quickly repeated the process with the other arm. Something stirred in his chest. The feeling of foreboding felt like life-or-death trouble, but at a point in the future. That should have alleviated his anxiety about his new queen risking herself being infected with Abraka's symbiont, but it didn't.

He double-checked the mechanism to make sure it was firing correctly and practiced targeting using the controls and then uploaded it back into place. He sent the unit back to the medical bay and took a deep cleansing breath. This would work. It had to work.

The door slid open for Calen. "I have heard our new queen is taking us to war."

"I suppose you could say that."

His brother continued rambling. "She's ambitious, this queen of yours. She is also a clever queen, for she has plans inside of plans. With her new protector at her side, the warriors believe she will always be victorious. Is it true that she named you her takadon?"

"She did, and we solidified our bond already."

"I can see why the elders have formalized her as our queen of queens moving forward. The new uniform designates our line as the takadon of the one who rules us. I can't wait to get my uniform upgrade. It will get me noticed among the new queens."

Ignoring his sibling's silly talk, Larok sighed. "I do not believe she understands why we were given uniforms with the new symbol that represents the joining of Draconian and human bloodlines."

Calen responded automatically. "She was the first to accept a Draconian mate and she will forever be thought of as our queen."

"Do you think queens have the capacity to care for others in the same manner as warriors?"

"Don't tell me you are falling in love with your queen, Larok. I thought you were smarter than that. She will eventually take another breeder to her bed. Regardless of what they say, it is what they all end up doing. Even being her heart mate will not save you from that fate, my hatchling mate."

"My Hope is refusing to entertain the idea of creating a stable of breeders. Humans wish only for the number of young they can care for with their own two hands."

"I noticed from the information in the Zelerian database that Queen Cassandra chose a lone warrior and he was no breeder, yet she was smiling and happy. Perhaps human queens require less to be satisfied."

"I believe that is true. Will you do me a favor?"

"I would do anything, for you, your new queen, and your little one. You know that, Larok."

"I want you and Kalar at my side when we board Lakara's vessel. I looked over the information in the database during the meeting. They got through her personal shielding with an endless volley of laser fire. I feel this is perhaps the way to defeat the young queen on the trading vessel. I wish the three of us to spread out behind Lakara and concentrate our fire on bringing down her shield."

"I will speak with Kalar, and we'll meet you in the medical bay shortly."

Nodding, some of his anxiety eased. "Thank you, Calen. I sense some danger, so we must be careful."

"I sensed it as well. We will be vigilant."

HOPE

In the armory, Hope held out both arms as they fitted her body with lightweight armor. It was molded to her specific form and placed between her under things and the fancy new uniform. "We are putting one weapon in each sleeve. Each will hold one poison dart. You lift your arm, pull down on your wrist, and place your thumb on the round silver disk. I am filling each sleeve with plain darts right now, so you can practice your aim."

"I won't need them if Larok is at the controls. He's a really good shot."

Glancing up at her, he smiled slightly. "I am pleased that you favor my scion so heavily, but he is just one of many."

She lifted her arm and shot off an arrow, like he suggested. "Not to me. He's my one."

"Queens don't allow a single male to cleave to them. It is most unseemly. They have a collective of breeders."

"Yeah, your Draconian brothers in our sector were all confused about that as well. They tried sorting themselves into small family grouping of two warriors per queen. It didn't work out all that well for them. The women mostly kept picking individual warriors. There are a few tri-bonds, but not many."

"Tri-bonds?"

Shooting off another arrow, Hope was growing more sure about this plan. It felt right. "I guess that's what they came up with to describe small family groupings. Anyway, I'm happy with what I have."

Loading her with two more arrows, Jeron murmured, "We will see what the future holds, Queen Hope."

"Thanks for using my name, even if you did put that pompous descriptor in front of it."

"Perhaps I will grow more comfortable with such things when we arrive at our new home world."

Shooting off two more arrows, she came reasonably close to what she was shooting. "How long after the arrow hits the creature does the crusty critter stops trying to attack me?"

"It should be almost instantons. We included a strong nerve agent that should paralyze the symbiont, then it's down to however long it takes for the poison to take effect."

"This is going to work, right?"

"I suppose my scion told you of our line." Snapping the two poison darts into place, he looked down at her. "I feel danger but not death is in store for you. Do not let my words make you careless, Queen Hope. The future is ever-changing. Just because I sense something is no guarantee it will come to be."

"I understand. I have a good gut feeling about this as well."

She placed a hand on each of the older man's arms and found herself becoming emotional. "We're going to be family, you and I. Together, Larok and I will continue your line. How do you feel about that?"

Finally the smile that had been trying to break free spread across his face. The horns flicked back and forth slightly on the normally taciturn man's head. "I am more pleased than I have words to say. Though we may not always agree, the challenges make each of us the better for it."

"Good, because I want all of us to stay close and visit a lot with each other. Soon your other sons will have mates. I'm excited about our little ones growing up together. Family is really important to me."

"Family is important to us as well. I can hardly imagine all my scions with mates."

"I have a question. How many warriors are on that trading vessel?"

"I would expect around three hundred, give or take a few."

"Add that three hundred to the thousand on board this vessel, and we've got just about enough to settle our own little world if Queen Cassandra doesn't accept us."

"Either way means freedom, Queen Hope. It is nice to have options."

Larok entered the room, looking a little anxious. "Are you ready, my queen?"

She nodded and walked over to him. "They gave me poison darts. How cool is that?"

Frowning, he responded. "They should be at the same temperature as the rest of the room."

Jumping onto her tip toes, she whispered in his ear. "Yeah, I learned all about the laws of thermodynamics in school too. I really love you, though." Giving him a playful kiss on the cheek, she pulled back.

He leaned his forehead down to touch hers. "I love you as well, my Hope. Be very careful and do not take any chances with your safety." After a moment of bonding, they both went their separate ways.

Having Larok covering her back was the one thing that made this possible. Hope steeled herself for the confrontation that was to come. Standing outside the door to the medical unit, she took a deep breath and the door slid open. She stepped over the threshold and began rummaging around. When she walked by the stasis unit, she turned it off, fiddled around with some more buttons, and picked up a data pad. Trying to look nonchalant, she walked across the room and sat on a stool with her back to the dying queen.

Though every survival instinct she had was screaming at her to run, she shifted in her seat, pretending to swipe though information on the pad. Hearing a slight noise, she glanced up at the security camera nearest her position. Unable to stand the waiting, she stood and pivoted around. Sure enough, the creature had shifted position, becoming a more noticeable bulge in her stomach area. She appeared almost pregnant.

She pretended not to notice, even though she didn't think her behavior mattered because the queen's eyes were still closed. The creature relied upon its host to see and hear.

Being in such a dangerous predicament, made her think of things she hadn't considered. What was the probability of hitting the queen accidentally with a poison arrow while trying to kill the creature? It was pretty high, she imagined. Moving to one side of the room, she leaned against the wall, feeling more confident that she could get the proper angle if she needed to. She folded her hands over her chest and waited anxiously.

A chill crept up her spine when there was a strange sloshing sound. Hope turned in time to see a small rip open from the inside of the soft flesh of the older queen's body. The tear was on her side, under the ribcage. When the symbiont slithered out of her body, Hope was shocked. Like elder Thermon has theorized, the creature was gigantic. It must have grown down her extremities and taken up all the extra space in her body.

The symbiont looked like a large animal bladder of some sort. It was a sickly white color. Instead of arms and legs, it had long stringy tendons that looked like they may have embedded in tissue because they had blood and bits of sinew hanging off each one. It suddenly made all kinds of sense. Since the queen was ancient, the symbiont had been growing all that time inside her. It would have to be large. It made her wonder if the creature was like some kinds of fish back on Earth who only grew as large as their fish tanks permitted.

As it rose to his full height, Hope realized that trying to save Queen Abraka might not have been one of her better ideas. There was no way. The elder queen looked almost hollowed out. There was no possible way she could survive the removal of the symbiont.

Suddenly, the creature was moving quickly, flying across the room at her. Raising both hands, she shot off both of her darts directly at the bulk of the strange creature. They didn't even slow it down.

Hope would have to be crazy not to notice that it was a distant relative, a sort of first-cousin-twice-removed of the squid from the raider. She scooted back as far as she could before seeing it torn in two by laser fire. Larok continued shooting until there was nothing but scorched metal floor. It smelled disgusting.

The door flew open, and the medics ran straight to the elder queen. Jeron rushed to her side. "We watched on the monitors. It was much larger than we anticipated. It seemed sentient, had a mind of its own and moved of its own free will. Even after watching the informational video, I didn't understand until it rose."

Placing a reassuring hand on his shoulder, she nodded. "It surprised me as well. It looks like Larok destroyed it all."

Glancing towards the dark stain on the floor, Jeron nodded. "The smell is thoroughly revolting."

Kalar tossed aside his medical scanner, shaking his head. "She never would have survived even a surgical removal. The symbiont was simply too large and deeply rooted in her system."

Jeron hauled in a deep breath. "Activate the stasis field in case remnants were left behind. We'll jettison her body properly before we leave this sector of space. Sanitize the room. I'll not risk exposing countless worlds in Naxis space to this particular contamination."

Just then Larok burst into the room. Working his way around the scorched mess on the floor, he came to her first. Hope didn't waste any time throwing herself into his arms. "Thanks for killing that dammed thing. My poisoned arrows didn't seem to have an effect at all."

"I saw that. Are you well?"

"I feel like absolute garbage because we couldn't save Queen Abraka. It would have been nice to know the real queen for a bit before she passed."

Pulling her close, he murmured. "You have a kind and compassionate soul."

Taking a deep breath, she put some space between them. "We still need to draw the notice of Queen Lakara.

Since Abraka can't give us any pointers, do you have any idea how we can do that?"

Easing her out of the room between them, Larok and Jeron left the medics to sterilize the room. The commander spoke. "I have been thinking on this. I believe we should send a covert message to her ship. We will say that our queen has passed and request a new queen."

They entered the elder's meeting room. Larok added, "My sire is correct about this being our best option. Our mother ship is in optimal condition, but older than many others in this sector. Only a young queen would see it as a worthy prize. Her ship is closer than the others, so she will get here first."

Hope rolled her eyes. "How convenient that she's in such close proximity to an elder queen in such poor health. It's almost like she was waiting for your sickly queen to die, so she could pick over her leavings. She'll probably be even more eager now that we are getting ready to harvest resources."

Surprised noises came from around the room. Elder Thermon chirped a frustrated sound. "This is why we need a queen. I am certain that you are correct, Queen Hope. None of us could have envisioned such a thing. You think like a queen, and that makes you the best choice in leadership for our people."

Tossing the older man a smile, she replied, "Aren't you a charmer? I have every reason to suspect some lucky woman is going to snap you right up."

"Again you are correct. I am chosen by a lovely and fascinating age mate. It happened so fast, I hardly knew what to make of it."

"Since I am only aware of one who would be your age mate, shall I guess that it is Queen Marion?"

Unable to contain his delight, he nodded, folding his hands in front of him. "Indeed it is."

"You have my most sincere congratulations. She is a really sweet lady."

"Thank you, Queen Hope."

Reaching out to touch his hand, she beamed at him. "We are mired in troubled times. It's wonderful to hear news good enough to lift our spirits."

"Thank you. Having an understanding queen to spend my evenings with adds an entirely new dimension to my life. I am more motivated than ever to see this mission succeed.""

"Glad to hear it." Turning to Jeron and Larok, she asked, "Are we ready to destroy a moon?" Hope couldn't believe she just asked that question. This whole experience was getting to be surreal.

Jeron gave them an informal report. "We have everything in place. Our particle weapon is fully charged, and the shuttles are ready for the harvest. Once we discharge the particle weapon, it should take about eighty microns for the explosion, another sixty before it is safe for the shuttles to enter the debris."

"We have to time this just right. How long will it take her to reach us at maximum speed?"

Jerod referenced his hand-held device. "A little over a hundred microns."

"Let us get started while we are still refreshed. We can all be in free space inside of the next twenty-four hours."

The commander asked, "Would you like to monitor from the bridge?"

"Until it's time to board the training ship, I think that would be a good idea. I want Larok with me, not out participating in the harvest."

Placing his hand-held back into its receptacle on his utility belt, the older warrior looked from her to his scion and back again. "A queen's takadon remains at her side always. Do not allow anyone to convince you otherwise. I suspect it is why Queen Cassandra's mate never leaves her side."

Letting out a relieved sigh, Hope let herself relax a little. "That's good to know. Let's get this job done and get the hell outta this sector of space."

Once they were all on the bridge, Jeron assumed his normal position at the primary panel. Hope sat beside Larok who was in front of screen scanning the surrounding area, rather than in his normal seat at the navigational array. "The training ship is holding in sector B-Five-Eight."

"Discharge particle weapon as previously programmed."

"Weapon discharge sequence initiated, sir." The warrior sitting at the weapons array was one she barely recognized, but he seemed intent on seeing to his task.

They watched the weapon launch and disappear for a moment. The first sign of destruction was the slow breaking apart of the moon, which for one split second Hope thought looked almost graceful, like a ballet of rocks. Then there was a huge explosion, with bits flying in every direction.

Hope asked anxiously. "Are we far enough from the blast?"

Larok assured her in a serious tone. "We have done this many times, my Hope. We carefully calculated the maximum safe distance, and then added a safety buffer of eight percent."

"Thank God. I've never seen anything like this before."

"Few on your side have, especially if the queens do not harvest in this manner."

Staring at the brutal destruction, Hope responded quietly. "I could be wrong, but I honestly don't think any of us would consider doing anything this destructive to harvest even very valuable resources."

When there was nothing but floating chunks of moon, Larok spoke. "We are counting down twenty microns until it is safe to enter the debris field."

They watched the floating bits slowly expand out and drift aimlessly in space. Jeron glanced in her direction. "I believe our harvest will be extremely rich. I'm reading larger quantities of about thirty valuable gemstones, metals and other elements."

Hope sighed. "We might need every single advantage we can get by the time this is said and done."

Larok sounded off. "It is time to contact the training vessel."

His father reached for the console and keyed in some information by hand. "We will contact them by audio on our encrypted frequency."

Within moments a crisp voice came over the com. "I'm here, my sire."

"Brex, I need you to listen carefully. Do as I ask and nothing more."

The warrior's voice changed, taking on a wary tone. "I understand."

"Our queen passed shortly after our harvest began. We are in need of a new queen. I wish you to relay that message to Queen Lakara."

There was a slight delay. "You wish me to alert her that you are in need of a new queen?"

"I will explain later, but do as I ask. Also let your hatch-mates know the exact words I have spoken."

"We will be ready, my sire."

The moment Jeron closed down the connection, Hope commented. "His response was odd. Why did he say they would be ready?"

"The phrase, *do nothing more* is code that we are planning to attempt to retrieve them from Lakara's ship. They will be waiting at the docking port for us. We created a stasis field cage to trap her in."

"That ought to just about do it. I'll just lure her into the trap, and then we'll get the hell outta here."

Larok spoke. "It looks like a natural distortion is forming. It will take our scientist a few moments of scanning it to key it to the exact coordinates of Naxis."

Jeron opened his com channel. "Launch shuttles. Just like always, focus upon harvesting the largest chunks first. We will spread an energy net and pull through what we can as we clear the debris field."

About a hundred little dots lit up along the top of the view screen. Hope watched as they began moving forward, a few at a time. The shuttles began swarming the debris field. Huge bot arms came out and began grabbing clumps of debris. She assumed they knew what they were looking for. Maybe the shuttles had scanners or something along those lines. She marveled at how similar the bot's arms were to the ones that fixed stuff on the ship. Watching them take load after load to the mother ship, her head spun as she wondered not only how they chose but how they unloaded so fast, and where in the world would they store so much rubble on the ship?

"The red dot is your queen friend Sinthia." Larok enlarged the dot multiple times until she would see an actual shuttle. Tilting her head slightly she watched it moving gracefully through the front of the debris field. Large arms kept reaching out to grab pieces of debris and then stowed them in the underbelly of the shuttle. "She's very efficient."

Larok looked over his shoulder. "The training ship has turned and is moving towards our position."

Hope leaned over to look at his monitor. "This plan is going a lot smoother than I imagined."

His eyes found hers, and she saw how worried he was about having her involved in the mission. Rather than speak his mind about it again, he glanced away. "We must prepare for the boarding. I aim to ensure this mission is executed precisely as planned."

AFTER GOING OVER THE SPECIFICS OF THE PLAN ONE more time, they loaded themselves on a stealth shuttle with thirty warriors. The atmosphere was tense, as it normally was when two queens engaged in a face-to-face confrontation. Larok suddenly began doubting the wisdom of boarding Lakara's ship. Without thinking, he wrapped his wing around Hope and pulled her closer to him.

Stroking his wing gently, she said, "Everything's going to be all right. We can do this."

It felt strange to have a queen pay so much attention to him that she could figure out what he was feeling. "I will not allow you to be harmed. Trust me to guard your safety."

"Don't be a hero, Babe. We go in, we stick to the plan, and we get out. I don't like surprises."

The shuttle jerked slightly as the docking ring sealed. The ring opened, and the ladder slid down. Calen climbed up first and helped their new queen up. Larok followed quickly, to find Brex and Tabor gaping at his queen. Drawing her into the circle of his arm, he made introductions. "Queen Hope, Brex, Tabor, and Malox are my siblings. Greetings brethren. I have been selected, and this is my new Queen. Her name is Hope."

Brex spoke first. "Greetings, Queen Hope, we welcome you to the *Raspian*." Grasping Larok's shoulder, Brex frowned. "It is pleasing to see you again, Larok. I did not think to set eyes on you ever again."

"My queen insisted upon retrieving you."

The man's eyes roamed over his uniform and then searched his face. "You are now takadon to your new queen?"

Nodding, Larok grasped his other arm. "We have no time to talk of such things."

Shooting a curious glance at Hope, he stated sternly. "You should not have brought a queen here. Lakara will challenge her, and your slight queen does not look like she has even a small chance at besting such a formable opponent."

"I'm glad you see her as weak. We are counting on Queen Lakara making that mistake as well. I have much to tell you, but there is no time. You must trust me."

"I am with you, my brethren, no matter the costs."

"We have a plan for neutralizing Lakara. Once that happens, we will use a wormhole generator that we pulled from an alien ship to get us to free space. Our elders have planned all the details, and it will succeed if we work together."

"Of course we will do the elders' bidding. I cannot believe Queen Abraka passed, and you secured a strange alien queen so quickly."

"We have a hundred queens on the mother ship, all eager for warriors to breed with. Right now we must prepare for Lakara's coming."

Larok and his brothers rushed around setting up the

trap in the huge docking bay. The other warriors pushed all the cargo back against the wall. Grabbing Brex's electronic tablet, he opened a channel and turned it around to Hope. "I have loaded a translation program. It will enable her to understand your words."

"Queen Lakara, I request an audience to speak with you."

Lakara's face came up on the screen. She was very young, Draconian, and had very large dark eyes. Her face was contorted into a mask of fury. "You dare to breach the security of my ship?"

Hope lifted her chin in an effort to look authoritative. "I wanted to come over and pay you a little visit. I wish to shake hands with your symbiont and see how she's enjoying her new home."

The other woman's eyes got large. "What did you just say to me?"

"I was just explaining how your big secret's out in the open now. We know your kind has been preying on Draconian queens for thousands of years. That's going to stop as of today."

"You lie, little alien queen. And you will die slowly for daring to speak such words out loud."

Preening a bit, Hope replied, "On my world, I'm a really strong warrior. They train us from the time we can walk to kick serious ass."

"What do you hope to gain by coming here?"

"I'm taking this ship. If you want to stop me, give it your best shot."

Screaming in frustration, Lakara slammed her hand on the com. When the screen went black, Hope glanced up at Larok. "How do you think I did? Is she mad enough to come and challenge me?"

Brex spoke up. "I think Queen Lakara is enraged. Are you really a fierce warrior?"

Holding out her arms, Hope asked, "Do I look like warrior to you? If I can be accused of having a super skill, it's clearly talking total crap to people who can tear me limb from limb."

"You said you had a plan, Larok. This does not sound like a good one."

"Trust me, all will be well. We know what we're doing."

A young queen's voice said, "Well, I'm not convinced that's true. This looks like a total clusterfuck to me." There was a flapping sound, and when Larok turned, he saw the mimic open his wing from around the small queen named Sinthia. They had camouflaged themselves into the side of the wall.

Larok's frustrated voice sounded off. "You should not be here, Queen Sinthia. The danger level is high."

His queen agreed. "Get back into the shuttle, Sinthia."

She pulled out a laser pistol, she charged it with a flick of her thumb. "Well, that's where you're wrong. Vxion and I are getting back to free space no matter what. That depends on the success of this mission."

"You're a distraction we don't need."

"I don't really care. If you're distracted, that's your problem."

"March you ass back onto that shuttle, or I'll have the warriors pick you up and carry you."

"You don't know much about warriors if you think for a hot minute they'd do something like that. In their world, queens solve their own problems through physical combat."

"I'm not fighting you, knucklehead. I'm trying to protect you."

"That's almost funny." She slammed her laser pistol

back into its housing on her waist and pulled out an old-fashioned *batlet*. She shook it open, twisted the rings on both sides of the handle, and blades slid out of each end. "The thing is, I'm what you pretend to be. My father spent years training me in advanced weapons and hand-to-hand combat. I'm the only person here who's actually fought a Draconian queen and won. So, we'll be doing this my way."

"We only have another couple of minutes."

"You keep her busy talking. Vxion and I will try to blast and cut through her shielding. We listened in on your plotting and planning, so we're clear on trying to maneuver her into the stasis field. We'll press her forward into position. Remember her shield has to come down for the stasis unit to be effective. All you have to do is keep backing up to position her in place. The others will keep her warriors off us. Like you said, we work the damn plan."

Larok spoke up. "Lakara is probably listening to every word we just said."

Stepping forward, Sinthia replied cheerfully. "That's the beauty of our new revised plan. If she walks through that door, she battles it out like a true queen. If she turns tail and runs, we'll let every queen in the Draconian fleet know that she was too cowardly to face a weak human in defense of her territory. I almost forgot, if she can't be taken, she is not to be given the opportunity to escape. We kill her and scorch her dead body to cinders on the floor."

Queen Hope stood gaping at the young queen. "Damn, what in the hell happened to you?"

Testing her batlet in her hand, the younger queen shrugged. "I grew up in the black of space. It's a harsh life and sometimes you have to be ruthless if you want to survive. We've got over a hundred and twenty women counting on us to get them home. Honestly, I was made for days like this."

Hope finally let the annoyed expression slip from her face. "Is this the point where I'm supposed to bray about how it's a good day to die? I gotta say, I'm really not feeling that one."

Brex commented admiringly, "Two queens with fire in their gut to match their fiery strands."

Queen Hope quipped, "He means hair."

The younger queen chuckled and rolled her eyes. "I've spent a lot of time on the Draconian home world. There's nothin' you can teach me about a warrior that I don't know."

The door to the loading bay creaked open to reveal Queen Lakara and a horde of her warriors. "I should have expected to be betrayed by the scions of Jeron. You are all traitors, and you will pay with your lives for betraying your queen. I will hunt down every single warrior in your line, and the last thing they will see is my face as they bleed out."

Hope stepped in front of Larok. "Don't even look at him. You talk a lot of smack for a slimy symbiont who can't even see, smell, or speak without a real live person's body to help you."

Sinthia and Vxion slowly backed away, flanking Lakara. Larok's crew surged forward to the back of the loading bay, near the door. They would engage every one of Lakara's warriors who entered the room.

"If you think we value one skin suit above another, you are wrong. One body is much the same as another to us."

"I noticed that. Queen Abraka's symbiont tried to jump from the dying queen to me. Want to guess how that worked out for her?"

Lakara bared her teeth. "Abraka was the oldest among us."

"Not anymore. My takadon scorched her vicious ass to the floor. When we left the room, only a black stain on the metal ground was left as evidence that she ever existed."

"You will die screaming in pain for daring to touch a Vithacan."

"Is that what you call your species? It's nice to put a name to the face, not that you really have faces. Only people have those. Vithacans are more like a bizarre fungus of some sort."

"We are evolved. You are little more than the livestock upon which we feed."

"You sound a little like a soul-sucker."

Stepping forward, Lakara shifted her batlet from one hand to another. "We hate that disrespectful term."

"Jesus, you *are* soul-suckers. I guess that explains why you're all so damned vicious. You get off on the hormone cocktail humanoids release when they're scared, don't you? If I remember my science, it's partly cannabinoids and opioids. Must be quite a party for you."

Lakara's chin lifted defiantly. "Terrified is the descriptor you're looking for, frail queen. The more intense the emotion, the more potent and pleasurable the feeding becomes."

Hope lifted her batlet up and casually tucked it behind her head, leaning her wrists over the top of each end. "That's some seriously sick shit. You know that, right?"

"You do talk and talk and talk. In truth, you speak brazenly for a being with no fighting skills."

Smiling pleasantly, Larok's queen preened a bit. "I like to talk. You're a pretty good conversationalist for a demented freak."

Lakara's face lit up with the most malevolent look he'd ever seen on a queen's face. Not taking his eyes off Lakara,

Larok tried to shove down all the fear, anxiety, and self-doubt the queens had spent a lifetime teaching him. His queen was protective of him. The knowledge that there were queens willing to stand between a warrior and certain death—it soothed his soul. When he moved into a better position, he saw his brothers were trying to work their way around behind Lakara, but she hadn't come fully into the room yet. There were a thousand ways this could go bad. His anxiety level kicked up a notch when Lakara and Hope renewed their verbal altercation.

Lakara sensed movement and her head snapped over to pin him with a hate-filled glare. "So, he's your favorite? I'll make certain he suffers the most."

"You all say the same stupid thing when you're trying to strike fear in the heart of your opponent. You know that, don't you?"

Lakara lowered her chin, and her gaze turned deadly. His new queen didn't give her time to respond before continuing her taunts. "It's really funny how Draconian queens think they're all unique but warriors are all the same. It's just the opposite. Warriors are all subtly different. Draconian queens all look alike, think alike, and fight just alike. I'm guessing you're all too preoccupied with feeding off the fear of your warriors that you don't take the time to properly care for the body you inhabit. Then again, I'll bet if we pulled you all out of your hosts and lined you up, we wouldn't be able to tell one from the other."

Lakara stared at her for a moment. "This doesn't have to end with your head on my batlet, little queen. You are clever and resourceful. Our fleet would welcome you." Glancing around, she shrugged. "Perhaps they will even let you keep my training ship."

Hope laughed. "You think I want to fly around this

godforsaken sector of space, battling it out with every queen we come across, just to protect a ship—and do what? Try to enjoy blowing up innocent world after world in a never-ending quest for riches? Don't be absurd. Humans would consider that half of a life, at best."

"You know nothing of true honor, of the responsibility of carrying on your species in the face of impossible odds." Waving her hand around at the males around her, her voice turned harsh. "You seem to believe warriors are beings of worth. They were created for our use, nothing more."

"Oh, I understand more than you think. You're a liar by the way. You lie about everything. You know the other queens would never accept a weak human in their midst. Also, the Draconians were just unfortunate enough to encounter a soul-sucker. Though you may have adapted them a bit, you did not create them."

"It matters not whether they were found or made, the fact remains that they serve us because we are superior. Here we rule, small alien." Taking a step closer, Lakara pulled up her batlet. "This is the weapon of choice for queens who consider themselves honorable. You can't know how much I hate seeing one in your weak little hands. You are perhaps the most unworthy creature I have ever laid eyes on."

"Yeah, and through your own arrogance and stupidity you are squandering good opportunities. Look around you, Lakara. There are a thousand different pleasures to be had, on an infinite number of worlds. Think about all the inter-esting new tastes, textures, and sights you are missing out on when you blow a planet out of the sky. Not to mention interesting new beings, who might be companionable mates and enhance your genetics. Maybe there is something even more pleasurable than fighting and sucking the life from innocent beings. Your kind will never know what you might have become, because you're too focused in wallowing in the filth you have made of this sector."

Larok could tell his new queen struck a nerve. Lakara growled and charged forward a few more steps.

"You know nothing of our struggles. We have carved out a home for ourselves here, and I will not let you spoil it. You think warriors are valuable, yet what you speak in their presence guarantees their death."

"Maybe we should send out a mass message to the fleet letting them know that alien symbionts rule all their queens. We have a nice little demonstration video that explains it. I wonder if your kind would survive. There is but one queen on each ship with a thousand warriors. They could gang up, vent you out an airlock, or any number of things."

"This you will not do." Taking another step, she slid the blades from her batlet. "If you think to get through my shield, think again. It is impenetrable."

Tilting her head, Hope replied curiously. "How do you know I haven't messaged them already?"

"You will die badly for this betrayal."

Hope took a step back. "I'm not sure I even know what that means."

Lakara moved forward, snarling her frustration. "I am a queen of queens, and you are nothing but a weak alien who..." Lakara stopped her endless verbal tirade. Sinthia and her warrior, Vxion, had darted forward from each side, shoving their batlets through her shielding. Lakara had to move deftly to keep the blades from touching her skin.

Hope turned her heirloom weapon on Lakara. "Yeah, that shield looks real impenetrable."

Larok pulled Hope back and flung her towards the shuttle. "The blades will never bring down her shield. We must concentrate our laser fire on the shield. Go back to the shuttle, my Hope. You are no warrior."

Once she took off running for the docking ring, he turned his attention to Queen Lakara. There was an all-out battle between the warriors. He rushed forward to attack from the front, careful to remember he was fighting the symbiont, not its host. Lakara was young, and if they could bring down her shield and take her alive, there was hope of removing the symbiont. Lakara's warriors were losing their minds because he and Vxion had joined the fight. Queens fought queens, that was Draconian law. For a warrior to turn on a queen was considered high treason, punishable by instant death.

He drew his laser weapon and joined Sinthia and Vxion. The three of them circled Lakara, concentrating their laser fire on her shield. A focused stun beam would have made neutralizing her a simple task. Unfortunately, Draconian queens wore a personal shield that no laser weapon or stun beam could easily penetrate. Therefore he did his best to lay down a continuous rain of laser fire, hoping to weaken her shield, while the other two concentrated their laser fire on each side.

Killing or disabling the symbiont while saving the host made for a nearly impossible task. Lakara swiped a batlet blade across Vxion's neck, creating a wound that could be deadly. Sinthia flew to his side. It was a clever move, as it took them both out of action.

Larok pulled out his other laser pistol and reloaded battery packs. Lakara turned on her one remaining opponent, the worthless warrior from the house of Jeron. Standing his ground, Larok fired one shot after another. There was some laser fire from behind her, and he knew it was his siblings trying to join the fight, but getting interrupted by her warriors. Lakara's shielding blinked, causing her to stop with a mortified expression on her face. When it did not fail, she pressed forward again. Larok did the only thing he could. He kept firing and reloading at such a rapid pace, his pistols were beginning to overheat.

Suddenly, Hope was at his side again. She'd apparently raided the weapons cabinet and come back with a laser rifle in addition to her heirloom weapon. She tossed him the laser rifle and pulled out her own weapon. Larok found he was grateful for her return, though deep in his heart, he wanted her a million parsecs away from this battle.

Standing shoulder to shoulder, they doubled down on the effort to rob Lakara of her protective shielding. Larok saw his brothers break away from the fighting to join them. The Draconian queen roared her anger when she realized she was getting fired on from all sides. The moment her shield blinked and then fizzled out, Calen caught her in the small of her back with his laser pistol. Thankfully, he'd remembered to switch the weapon to stun.

When she was down, Larok and Calen dragged her forward by the arms into the stasis field. Hope made a loud shrill sound by putting her fingers to her mouth, catching the attention of most of the warriors.

"Your queen is down. That makes me the victor. Lay down your weapons and submit to the rule of your new queen."

Though not happy with the outcome of the fight, they did as she commanded.

Sinthia's voice sounded off. "I hate to rain on your queenly parade, but we've got wounded. I need a medic right now." Two warriors came forward. Touching a now-empty ornamental bottle tied around her neck, she gestured to her warrior. "I shared my balm of power. It has strong healing properties, but it's not going to be enough."

One of the medics took out a stasis strip and laid it down on the warrior's body. "We will take him to the medical unit while you and the remaining queen continue the combat."

"We're not fighting. I don't care about being queen. Let's get him moving."

Hope nodded. "Thank you, Sinthia, and I hope all is well with Vxion."

The young queen jerked her chin like a warrior. "Get us the hell outta here. I want to go home."

Bowing playfully, his queen responded, "Your wish is my command, Queen Sinthia."

The young girl frowned. "You're a real funny lady."

HOPE

SITTING ON THE BRIDGE OF THE TRAINING SHIP WITH Larok at her side, Hope was eager to make it back home. So far Lakara's crew had been quiet and respectful to her, although it was clear they were not warming to Larok. She wasn't sure what that was about, so she kept her mind on the job.

Jeron's voice came over the com. "The rupture is diminishing instead of stabilizing. We will need to wait for it to collapse, or it might interfere with opening a clean wormhole. We will only get one shot at making it through, so we'll have to move quickly."

She responded, "We're in position and waiting for your go ahead."

Turning to look at Larok, she asked, "Did the shuttles return from harvesting yet?"

"Yes. I knew you would not wish to risk your warriors being outside the ship when we get the word to leave, so I told them to remain in place."

"I don't care so much about the loss of potential resources.

He responded quietly, "I well know your vigilance when it comes to issues of safety, but it didn't make sense to leave without them if there was time for at least one culling. We sent fifty shuttles, and each came back with a full cargo hold. I would say it was a good run."

Larok's brothers had taken up positions at the bridge panels. Brex spoke. "Queen Hope, we have another mother ship moving. It looks like she's leaving her sector and heading this way."

"Any idea who it is?"

"I believe it is Queen Stonara's ship."

"Tell me about her."

The man froze for a brief second. Larok spoke for him. "Stonara is an elder queen. Unlike Abraka, she is in good health. She has a reputation for being dangerous and ruthless. I would assess her threat level as high."

"How many warriors are on her ship?"

"At least a thousand."

"We can't save her, but we'll save her warriors if we can. Can we get a covert message to the warriors on that vessel?"

"We can. The elder warriors have been communicating between vessels for years."

"Send them Queen Cassandra's informational bulletin. Tell them to vent their queen and follow us into free space. If they cannot, we'll use both our ships to attack if she makes it through the wormhole."

Approaching one of the several open consoles, he responded promptly. "I'll see to it personally, my Hope."

An idea struck her brain fully formed, like lightning. "Play the bulletin on all ship's screens, so the warriors know what's going on."

"Yes, my queen."

"And Larok, right before we leave this sector, send an

encrypted file containing the message to every elder ship we can reach. I want every single warrior in this sector to know their queens are being controlled by the symbionts. We might not be able to save every warrior, but this at least gives them a chance to save themselves. Let them know that in one solar revolution we will create a wormhole for them to enter free space."

"Are you certain of this course of action, my queen. Once it is done, we have no way of taking it back."

"Would you leave your brethren in this sector ignorant of their own bondage?"

"I hesitate to answer that question. What you are suggesting will upset the entire order of our society. There is also a good chance that if the queens discover your message, they will make an organized attempt to enter free space as well."

"Sinthia once said that reward follows risk. Your brethren have been subjugated by the nameless symbionts for an endless age. I want to give them knowledge. What they chose to do with it is up to them. My gut tells me that they will spend the next year waging war to save the few remaining young queens on your home world."

"You are right, my Hope. Our young queens deserve a chance at being rescued. This is likely the only way that will happen."

Jeron's voice sounded over the com. "The wormhole has been initiated. It is growing and stabilizing. Move to within two parsecs and hold position until my mark, then follow us through."

"We have another queen approaching."

"By our calculations she has an eighty-two percent chance of being too late to make it through the wormhole."

"I'm sending an encrypted copy of the informational

bulletin to the all the elders within messaging distance. People on this side need to know what side's up."

There was a brief pause before he answered. "Agreed, Queen Hope. We're counting down twelve microns, then we head for the wormhole at maximum speed."

Hope responded crisply. "Understood. No insult intended, but I'll be glad to see the backside of Exion space."

She drummed her fingers on the console, turning things over in her mind. "I wish there were some way to tip the coming war in the favor of your brethren, my takadon."

Larok turned to look her in the eye. "It is admirable that you worry over the warriors we leave behind. It truly is. However, none of us know what the future holds, my queen. What I do know is, we have young to protect, and over a thousand warriors who have never know freedom, myself among them. We cannot tarry in this sector. Let us take our win today and revisit what we can do to help the ones we leave behind in one solar."

"Do you ever get tired of being right, babe?" Larok's face lit up in a brilliant smile. "Move us into final position to clear the debris field, as Commander Jeron asked."

"Yes, my queen."

When the cue from Jeron came, the ship accelerated behind the mother ship.

"Stonara's ship is bearing down on us. They jettisoned a life pod."

"Is it within scanning range?"

"Yes. There is only one life form inside. It is Queen Stonara. I don't know how they managed to get her into the pod but they did. The pod is caught in the planet's gravitational pull."

Excitement strummed through her chest at the thought

of rescuing yet more warriors. "I hope they make it through in time. There are another thousand warriors on that ship, and I want them in free space.

There was some lurching that reminded Hope of turbulence by old Earth aircraft, and then it was suddenly gone. Larok spoke. "Take us a safe distance from the event horizon. We do not wish for our Draconian brothers to come crashing into us as they enter our space."

The navigational officer did as Larok asked. Within moments the final ship came tearing through the wormhole. Watching it muscle its way through the diminishing void was nothing short of terrifying. Though they had their shields up, the wormhole was causing some type of lightning-like energy to spark along the surface of the ship.

"Larok, they're not going to make it. Any ideas on what we can do to help?"

"We could send out some towing lines from our grappler and try to pull them free."

"Do it now."

Another warrior spoke. "Grappler away, my queen."

They watched as huge magnetic claws closed around two parts of Stonara's former ship and began to pull. Suddenly, Jeron's ship was there as well with attached grapplers. It was all they could do to jerk the ship through before it was torn apart. Watching it finally break free, she jumped to her feet as the distortion crackled and popped closed. "That's the weirdest thing I've ever seen." Hitting a button on the console, she spoke. "Sinthia, this is Hope. Can you talk."

"I've been watching your big battle on the monitor down here in the medical bay. Congratulations."

"I'm not calling to chitchat. Can you take this ship, so I

can bounce over to the damaged ship and see what they need in the way of repairs?"

"They are warriors. They don't need us. When are you going to get that through your head?"

"Just call me a nosy bitch. I want to have a look at that ship."

"Knock yourself out. I'll hold down the fort here."

LAROK

Climbing up the docking ring into the second mother ship, Hope grasped Larok's hand, and he pulled her up the last step. "My goodness, can't we design shuttles to dock horizontally with the mother ship?"

An older male wearing a dark maroon form suit, answered immediately. "I will see the modifications are made immediately, my queen."

Palm-smacking her forehead, Larok's queen stammered, "Sorry, I forgot how literally new warriors tend to take statements like that."

The older warrior blinked at her, his face totally devoid of expression. Sighing, she tried again. "I'm not insinuating that you're not an experienced warrior or anything like that. I was just remarking that you are new to dealing with human women."

"As you say, my queen."

Shooting him an exasperated look, his pretty queen's shoulders sagged. "Larok, help."

Stepping forward he dipped his head respectfully to the older warrior. "I believe Queen Hope is simply remarking on how much more convenient it would be for queens if they did not have to climb ladders at such sharp inclines. Naturally, that is a minor problem for another day. Our priority must be on repairing the ship, so we can travel to our new home world."

Eyeing the emblem on Larok's uniform, he glanced at Hope for a moment before speaking again. "You are takadon to Queen Hope?"

"I am."

"You speak for her."

"Not usually."

Hope interjected. "He does speak for me. Please follow his directions like you would my own. Sorry, I'm such an incoherent mess today. What with the battle, and the harvest, and the escape into free space, it's just been a hectic day."

The older man took a small step back. "You are not like the queens we have known."

"Yeah, I get that a lot. Would it be possible to find a meeting room and a hydro pack and begin talking about repairs? I've asked the other two ships to maintain a holding pattern until we are all three ready to travel."

"One queen commands three vessels?"

"I suppose that's the extent of it. I have my takadon's father in charge of the *Obsidian* and a younger queen in charge of the training ship."

The man looked alarmed. "There is another queen?"

"We've got like a hundred and twenty-seven human queens on the other mother ship. Can we get on with finding a meeting room? I'm dead on my feet."

"Certainly. My apologies, Queen Hope." He gestured towards what was probably the door. They couldn't really tell for the throng of warriors blocking their path. As Larok knew they would, the mass of warriors parted to make way for their small boarding party.

"If I may ask, what is a father?"

Hope's hand flew to her mouth. "Sweet day in the morning, I've actually been speaking Draconian. I didn't realize until this moment. How long has that been going on, babe?"

"Since the day after your arrival, my queen. The neural upload must be extremely compatible with human physiology, because you seamlessly integrated our language into the proper speech pathways in your brain. You do at times resort to your own language when using words that carry a great deal of emotion for you. You often use the words father, mother, love, brother and you use a great many human terms in reference to my little hatchling."

Placing her hand on her chest, she shook her head. "I honestly didn't realize I was doing that. It would explain how Draconians who haven't had English added to their translation program can understand what I'm saying."

A door opened when they approached, revealing a nice sitting area and a large table with a dozen chairs. Hope headed for the table, clearly intent on talking business. Larok dropped into a seat right beside his amazing queen and took out his data pad. Hooking into the ship's mainframe, he pulled status reports from engineering, navigation, and weapons control.

"It looks like weapons are offline. Our engines are running on low charge, but fortunately navigation is still operational, my queen."

Leaning over to look at the information he'd pulled up, she started to speak then closed her mouth again. Folding her hands together on the table top, she looked around at the mostly older warriors.

"I think that I'm putting the cart before the horse. First of all, let me say thank you for taking the decisive action to rid yourself of the symbiont and following us to free space. In case you are not aware, you are now in Naxis. This is a gigantic region of space that includes dozens of worlds bound together voluntarily by an Intergalactic Council of Planets. My people are the most recent addition to the council. I'm from Earth. We have a population of several million people, mostly queens. Many of the queens on my home world are seeking mates. I and almost a hundred and thirty other queens were on our way to become brides of the Talador elite when our ship was attacked. Larok rescued me and his family helped me rescue the other queens."

Larok interjected, "Human queens are more docile and easier to get along with than the queens we have known, since none of them are infected with the symbionts. They are sweet and open to our warriors. You have nothing at all to fear from a human queen. They are benevolent and always operate with our best interests at heart."

His queen leaned over and gave him a soft kiss on the cheek. "You always say the nicest things. It's one of the things I like about you."

There were some soft shocked chirps sounding off, so Larok spoke again. "When I first met my queen, I was too suspicious of her motivations to allow her to know that I hatched a little one of my own. I feared she would have my scion destroyed or give him to another warrior, so she would not have to contend with him. Instead, she gained my trust and welcomed my scion into her heart. I know that it will take time for you to see how different the humans are, so I ask only that you give them time to prove themselves to you. Our new queens welcome your questions, and as you have probably noticed, they are all too willing to take time out of their busy day to speak with us."

His queen nodded. "It's all true. Anyway, in free space the first wave of Draconians have established a home world with a couple of thousand warriors and God only knows how many queens. I've seen videos of your new home world, and it looks to be a lush paradise. The women who have relocated there have had only good things to say. I mean to take you there. We can build a city of our own or join with your brethren, who have already build a sprawling modern city. The new home world is called Onello, and it's ruled by a human queen and her warrior. Queen Cassandra was the queen in the bulletin we sent to you. She's always encouraged women and men willing to contribute to their military to resettle there, so I'm almost a hundred percent sure she will welcome all of you with open arms. For us to make our way there, we must make repairs to this vessel. I'll not leave you stranded while you struggle to right your engines."

"I understand what you are communicating. We are low on supplies to repair our vessel."

"The other two ships may have the supplies you need. If not, I will send Queen Sinthia to the nearest planet in our trading confederation to purchase whatever you need."

"It will be as you say, Queen Hope. Shall we ready the queen's chamber for your use?"

"Larok and I prefer more intimate accommodations. We require little besides each other for comfort. I need to ask if this ship is safe for other queens and our little hatchling to come aboard."

"Certainly. All the life support systems are fully operational."

"In that case, I'm going to divide the queens evenly

among the three vessels. If we could ready the queen's chamber, they will be happy to share the large suite of rooms."

"Is having so many in one open space wise?"

Hope nodded. "We love to spend time with each other. I promise, they be will more upset if we isolate them in separate quarters. Just ready the chamber for about forty queens and assign a small team of assistants. As I said, our needs are few."

"It will be as you say."

"I have one more request. Since I plan to stay aboard this vessel for the voyage to Onello, I am requesting that one of my queen friends bring our little hatchling to this ship. Where we go, he goes. We will bring our own incubation system, but I wish it to be installed properly in one of the smaller suites. The queen accompanying our child is a healer with a specialty in caring for the health of small children. If you have any needs in that area, please let her know when she arrives."

The older man looked really confused.

"I feel like a complete fool, because I don't think I asked your name or introduced myself properly. I'm afraid that I was on dumb-ass automatic pilot and a little preoccupied with getting this ship moving. Let me correct that over sight right now. My name is Hope Burk, scion of Andrew Burk. As you already know, Larok is my takadon. He is also the scion of Jeron."

The older warrior spoke. "I am Qurod, scion of Serod. I am pleased to meet you, Queen Hope. Are you accepting additional breeders at this time?"

"Larok will be my only mate. Human women normally chose individual males or perhaps two. Rarely do we take on more males than that."

"Do you mind if I ask why your limit is two."

Seeing his queen's face pink up, Larok found that he was interested to hear the answer to that question himself.

"Well, I suppose that when we sleep, having a warrior on each side makes us feel safe. We are reasonably certain we can keep one or two males satisfied. Adding more than two divides our time and we feel we are depriving our males of companionship."

"You seem to give some care to the needs of your warriors."

"I promise that we do. Might I suggest that you introduce yourselves to the queens when they arrive? One of the elders on the *Obsidian* has already been selected. Perhaps you will obtain some reassurance from speaking with elder Thurmon and the commander of the *Obsidian*, Elder Jeron."

Elder Qurod shot him a curious look. "You have selected your takadon's sire to be your first?"

"Commander Jeron was already in that position when I took possession of the *Obsidian*. Since his performance was beyond reproach, I saw no reason to change it. If things aren't broken, I don't usually try to fix them."

"That is a wise way of seeing things. It will lower our crew's anxiety to know that you have no wish to change everyone's general duties. Do I have your permission to continue as usual?"

"Absolutely. If it isn't too much trouble I would ask that you keep me in the loop regarding repairs and any other important matters. You can speak to me or to Larok."

Larok added, "I have noticed that your food stock is low. If you like, I can work with my queen to find foodstuffs in this sector of space that are similar to what we are used to consuming. I will ensure that you are supplied as needed."

"Very well, Takadon Larok. Your offer is much appreciated. We will prepare quarters for the two of you and your newly hatched scion and make arrangements for the new queens. As soon as the engineers are finished making their recommendations and we match our needs with currently available supplies, we will message you what we lack to repair this vessel adequately. If you would like, you can use this space as an office for now, as I'm certain you will wish to coordinate with the other ships in your armada."

"Thank you, Elder Qurod. You have been more cooperative than I thought possible under the circumstances."

"Do you mind if I ask what you are planning to do with my scion, Queen Lakara?"

Shock rippled up Larok's spine. "That is why you were so eager to cast Queen Stonara aside and make a run for the wormhole. It makes sense that you would risk much to protect your own hatchling."

His queen reached out to cover the elder's hand with her own. "Do not worry. Your daughter is young. The symbiont has not had time to root itself into her body. Queen Cassandra was successful in removing the creature from another Draconian queen who was a little older than your daughter. As long as she is in stasis, the creature is not growing. We will have it removed as soon as possible upon arriving on Onello."

"I would like to see her stasis unit if it is all possible," Elder Qurod said.

"I can do better than that. I will have the unit brought onboard. You may claim it and see to her safety yourselves. I believe you would be more motivated than anyone else to ensure her stasis is not disturbed, for you wish the symbiont out more than anyone else. I have no wish to see any harm come to the young queen or to rob you of anything you hold dear.

Larok added, "We were careful to stun her when we took her captive. You will see from basic scans that she is not harmed. We knew that her words and actions were not her own."

Elder Qurod let out a relieved breath and appeared to be reining in his emotions. "My scion and I thank you for that kindness. I am beginning to believe in the fantasy that you describe as our new future. I pray that all you say turns out to be true."

"Take a shuttle and visit your daughter. Escort her to this ship yourself if it will make you more comfortable."

"I have no words to describe my gratitude."

Giving his hand a squeeze, she responded, "Trust me, none are needed."

Watching the warriors filing out of the room, Larok turned to his queen. "I believe they are slowly understanding that their lives are going to be better. Your decision to turn Lakara over to her family was a good one. It will build trust with my brethren who know nothing of our ways."

"I just wanted him to feel secure. The worst thing we can do is break families up."

"Do you worry that we've assumed more responsibility than we can successfully manage?"

Running her hand down his wing, her face scrunched up into a pensive expression. "I should probably worry about that. I honestly don't think we have. The difficult part was escaping Exion space in one piece. Even with the complication of executing a harvest, we managed without losing one single warrior. How hard can it be to repair a ship in friendly space and fly to Onello? We've got this, babe. I promise."

"I find myself craving a planet and a home, just as you describe it. It's the dream I never knew existed before now. Now that I have discovered it, I cannot stop myself from craving it."

Cupping his face with both hands, she kissed him lightly on the neck. "Before I met you, my life was pretty crappy. All I had were dreams. Life on a pristine new world with a hot husband and permission to have as many kids as I want was my most outrageous fantasy. Sitting here on this ship, with a hot Draconian mate, making decisions about how to best get us home surpasses everything I ever thought I could do with my life. Being able to help others and make a meaningful contribution to their lives is the best feeling in the entire world. None of that would have been possible if you hadn't made the decision to retrieve my life pod. You saved my life. You gave me the kind of life a human woman could only dream of. For that I will be eternally grateful."

Lifting her into his lap, Larok took enough liberties with his lovely human mate to get him vented into space if his Draconian brethren found out. His Hope clearly loved his touch. He strongly suspected that she would never turn him away, no matter the circumstances.

Her eyes were half closed, and her bottom lip was trapped between her teeth as his hands worked their magic, tearing their uniforms open. Wrapping his wings around them created a space safe from the prying eyes of anyone who might walk in. Hope moved closer, lowering herself onto his rod. Something about silently stealing a moment in the open during working hours really made his lust peak. Hope was getting excited. Her hands were everywhere, and her lips found his so quickly it took his breath away. He stood, walked over to the wall, and placed her back against it.

The moment the door slid open, Larok cursed himself for forgetting to lock it. The shocked elder froze in place, unable to take his eyes of them. Hope looked over his shoulder, breathless and naked. "Out! This isn't a sideshow."

The terrified man did an about-face and walked back out of the room. Larok rubbed his face up one side of her face and down the other before speaking. "Door, lock now. Cancel override protocols, and respond only to my voice signature." Peering down into his lovely queen's face, he whispered. "Now you are my hostage. See how you ended up back where you started when we first met."

Laughing at his antics, she rubbed her body against his muscular frame. "I'm thrilled at the upgrade. The Zelerians really weren't doing it for me, babe. You, on the other hand, are totally different matter. I'd let you have your sexy way with me anytime."

Lifting her, Larok drove her soft body back down on his thick rod. Making her moan was getting to be his new favorite hobby. Her expressions, movements and sweet sounds were addictive. The fact that she was compliant in his arms was a sexy bonus. Once her hands landed on his stiff horns, the sex turned into a frenzy of need as they worked together to bring each other to their fall.

LAROK

Standing in the queen's chambers of the new ship, his Hope looked every inch a queen. Since they were closing in on the new Draconian home world, she'd agreed to wear a proper gown. Thrilled, Tamen, who oversaw the wardrobes of all the new queens, had spared no trouble outfitting her in finery befitting her station. He draped a large ornamental chain around her neck and stood back to admire his work. "You look perfect to my eyes," he said.

Rolling her eyes, she grinned. "I think you're trying to outdo Queen Cassandra's groomers."

"If so, I have succeeded beyond my wildest dreams."

Ella rolled over on their sleeping platform and shoved her electronic tablet aside. "Tamen's right. You look stunning."

"As do you. I think Tamen always takes extra care of you because he's sweet on you." Ella blushed, bounced off the bed, and shared some space in front of the mirror with Hope. Running a hand down the front of her gown, Ella murmured, "Blue suits me, I think."

As the two of them chatted, Larok reflected on his lot in

life. Over the last few weeks, they had settled down into a comfortable routine. His queen's admiring eyes were forever on him. It made him feel valued and respected. Even now, she watched him moving around the room, gathering things he needed for an outing with his little one.

He watched her pluck their little one from his sleeping unit. As always, his tiny arms came out to reach for her. Seeing them together was a paradise he never thought to want before meeting his Hope. Dropping items in a small clear box, he attached it to a small hover board.

"Since being aboard the Draconian ships, I haven't seen warriors use anything but clear boxes. What's up with that, babe?"

"We create them from processed and sanitized waste products."

Hope laughed, and she pulled his son close to snuggle him. "Forget I asked."

Her friend-queen Ella teased, "You say that a lot."

Larok watched his little one rooting his face again his queen's soft face. They were sweet together. Pulling back the tiny infant, she gazed down at him fondly. "His fist is trembling. That means he's cold."

Pulling open the front of her gown, she placed him close to her body, before pulling the fabric close around his wiggling form.

Larok's voice was almost a whisper. "You shelter my little one in your arms and share your body heat with him?"

"Is that wrong? It's kind of how we handle our little ones on Earth."

Walking over, he pulled her close with his son between them. "No my queen, what you are doing is perfectly right. Shall we go?"

Nodding, she cupped her hand around the back of the

now-snoozing infant. They made their way to the landing bay and joined the collection of women and warriors waiting there.

"I am eager to see this new world populated by our people."

"Everyone on Earth says it's really beautiful."

As soon as the door opened on the loading bay, they saw her other queen friend, Stacy. She craned her neck to see his little one. "What do you have there, Hope."

"You ask that every time. You can't hold him. He's sleeping."

"Darn. Can I at least get a look at him?"

"Fine, but give him some space. He been up for hours, and I don't want him to be all irritated and cranky when we meet Queen Cassandra."

Hope pulled back the edge of her dress and cradled the babe in the crook of her arm.

"My God, he's perfect."

"You say that every time as well."

Stacy quipped, "Don't keep chiding me. You're the baby hog. You have this precious little one and another one on the way. How are you two not exhausted?"

Hope smiled as her other hand drifted down to cover the hatching bulge on her lower stomach. "We manage. Don't you worry about that. Go find your own hot warrior and make babies of your own. This little one is mine, mine, all mine!"

Stacy's eyes lit up. "I have been looking, don't you think I haven't."

"We had almost two and half thousand between the three ships."

"Well there's a bunch more here, and I want to meet every single warrior before I decide."

"I hope you're keeping a spreadsheet or something like that. Otherwise, you'll never keep them all straight."

Ella interjected quietly. "She does collect information about them and hoards it all in that data pad of hers. She never collects anything useful, only what they like to eat, if they're willing to learn to dance, and how good they are at kissing."

Stacy blushed, but before she could respond, the bay doors slid open and Ella added, "What are you hanging around here for? You know she's not going let that babe out of her clutches."

"I'm picking up what you're laying down on that one, El. Let's get out of here, and let them get on with meeting Queen Cassandra. I'm more interested in finding out if that hot husband of hers has any brothers."

Grabbing Tamen's hand Ella grinned. "We'll help you scout hot warriors."

"I do not like it when you speak for me, my queen." Tamen's normally polite voice held a hint of annoyance.

Ella pulled him down to whisper in his ear. Larok watched the warrior's face light up. He said, "Yes! I am a very good judge of warriors. I will find your friend all the best ones immediately."

Hope snuggled his little one closer, as they watched them hurry away. "A little reverse psychology does wonders to motivate a warrior."

Larok tried not to smile at his naughty queen. She was forever saying just what was on her mind. "Human queens seem to love younglings. If your friend queen wants young of her own, she will have to choose a breeder."

Hope murmured. "We call them husbands."

Chirping a happy sound, Larok replied, "I did forget that."

Slipping his wing around her shoulders, they stared down at the baby's sweet face. Hope ran her hand tenderly over the back of the infant's head. "He's really small. Human newborns are about four times his size."

"Our young grow quickly into strong warriors." Larok smiled when the little one's face scrunched up into a delightfully expressive pose before a tiny chirping laugh escaped from his mouth. "He's having happy dreams."

Hope glanced up at him. "I think most babies do."

"If not for you, he would have never had the experience of being free, much less loved by a queen mother. I am thankful that you defended the young queens and were thrown in the escape pod. That one act of heroism led to many more and to freedom for many of my Draconian brothers. I thank you for all that you have done."

"I never thought of myself as heroic. It's like Sinthia said, when the chips are down, we do what we must to survive. I'm just happy we all made it out alive."

"For a queen to take over three ships and conduct harvest without it costing the life of a single warrior is unheard of among our people. Our queens never take a warrior's life into consideration when making decisions."

"Your queens are probably really nice. It's those damn things living inside their bodies that's the problem."

"Still, I am grateful for my little one to be cuddled in your arms."

"Have you thought a name for him yet?"

"I have been thinking on this. Warriors prefer strong names, befitting a warrior. Do you have recommendations?"

"Well in ancient Earth myths, Gabriel was an angel who protected humans. And in ancient Greek mythology there was Ares, the god of war, bloodshed, and violence."

"Ares sounds like Akes which was the consort to our goddess, Entares."

"Are we going with Ares or Akes?"

"I think, Ares, in honor of his human queen mother's god."

Looking down their sleeping hatchling, Hope noted, "Ares fits him. Even with his sleepy little horns curled down around his head, he looks like a fierce warrior. He has your strong jawline too. I love that."

"You are perceptive, my queen. I believe it is time for us to descend the ramp. I know you have clearly in mind what you wish to say to Queen Cassandra."

Wrapping one arm through his, they began moving forward. Hope wasn't used to all the pomp and circumstance. He could tell she was becoming more comfortable being a real queen. The warriors they brought from Exion were very persistent about following decorum. Out of respect, his Hope fell into line. Larok knew that she liked it best when it was just the two of them with his little one.

HOPE

ONCE THEY WERE SETTLED IN THE BANQUET HALL, Hope leaned forward, smiling at Queen Cassandra. "Somehow, you are not how I expected you to be."

"You thought I would be much more formal."

Nodding, Hope acknowledged it was true. "I did. Somehow I forgot, we queens are only human."

Taking a drink of her wine, Cassandra eyed her curiously. "Word has come to my ears that you wish to establish a planet of your own. Is this true?"

Stopping with a pincher full of food halfway to her mouth, Hope put it down again. "I am of two minds about it. On the one hand, what if a Draconian queen figured out how to access the Naxis? She could destroy our entire planet and every person on it. They are quite capable of doing that. If that happened, no warriors would get to enjoy their freedom. Too many warriors gave their lives for the few who have escaped to risk them all in one place."

"This I have considered as well."

"On the other hand, we are few. If we split ourselves into two groups, we are all the weaker for it."

"Again, you are correct. Though you have doubled the number of warriors on this world, five thousand is still very few in the general scheme of things."

"I have discussed with my warriors what they wish, and it seems either a continent on this world or founding a new home world. It seems they are excited about being free and wish to establish their own elder counsel with a ruling queen."

"I'm inclined to keep us together for now. We can share queenship of this world."

"This is an offer I would accept."

"You will make a good queen, and if anything happens to one of us, our people still have one in reserve."

"Heaven forbid any ill should come to you, Queen Cassandra. That would never be my wish. In the beginning, I did not think myself worthy or capable of being a queen to so many warriors. The more challenges we faced, the more I came to realize that perhaps I have something to offer after all. Now, I find myself drawn to leadership. Because I have relied on so many warriors, I feel responsible for seeing to their welfare. To do that, I must have some authority. I'm sure you know better than most that leadership is more duty than pleasure, especially for those of us who do not crave power for its own sake."

The other woman smiled. "You have been around warriors so much that you speak like a warrior. That happened to me as well. I was a refugee from Earth one moment and a queen the next. Like you, luck and circumstance pulled me into this role. Yet, I would not change it even if I could."

Hope's voice warmed to the older woman. "In that, we are alike."

Queen Cassandra's expression lit up. "We both chose

simple warriors as our one. This is another thing we are like-minded in."

"I did notice that. Perhaps I was just following your good example."

Laughter spilled forth from Cassandra's mouth. "I somehow doubt that. I think I was trauma-bonded to my Mathadar in the beginning, because he was the one who took me from the Strovian vessel. I realized somewhere along the way that it was much more than that."

"It's strange that you say that. My experience was similar. Since Larok was the one to save me, I clung to him at first."

"That is all in the past, my new friend. Now, we must focus on rebuilding our world. Shall I assume we will share one military?"

"Of course. We agree to the two mother ships being used in defense of our new home world, under your mate's command. However they will be crewed by our warriors and I accept responsibility for supplying the vessels and seeing to their maintenance. We consider them our property. Therefore, should we part ways at some time in the future, they will be used to ferry us to our new world and provide for planetary defense."

Hope explained, "Truth be told, I see them as the property of my warriors, so they are not mine to give."

"What of the training vessel?"

"My warriors have bestowed that upon me as an heirloom of my line."

Looking over the embellishments of queenship her warriors had woven into the design of Hope's dress and jewelry, Queen Cassandra nodded her approval. "I did notice that you have been awarded the symbols of a new royal line, one of mingled Draconian and human blood. I am given to understand it is quite an honor among the Draconians."

"My warriors seem very traditional compared to the ones you rule."

"Perhaps they see it as a reward for bringing them to free space."

Hope waved her hand through the air. "That was more of a group effort, but I did my share to see us to safety. I think of the trading vessel less of a royal flagship, and more of a mechanism for moving our population to and from other worlds for diplomatic missions, and quite honestly, trade missions, until we can purchase a proper freighter. You are more than welcome to accompany me, or borrow it for missions of your own. You will find my warriors competent and resourceful."

"You did not describe them as obedient, which is the descriptor most often associated with Draconian warriors."

Hope beamed. "To be quite honest, I have done my very best to combat their tendency towards blind obedience. I feel it diminishes our males and claws at their dignity. We have even developed a bill of rights for the warriors I lead."

The older woman's eyes narrowed. "I noticed you used the term 'rule' in reference to me, and 'lead' in reference to yourself. I'm not sure how I feel about that."

Refusing to get into a debate about the finer point of their very different styles, Hope elected to change the subject. "Would you like to see my little Ares? He's really adorable."

"Yes please. Little ones are a never-ending source of fascination to me."

"How many children do you have, Queen Cassandra?"

"Mathadar and I have been a breeding pair for coming up on four years now. He hatches continuously every three months. I can't begin to guess how many we have. I stopped naming them two or three years ago. We simply ran out of names."

Hope nailed her with a disapproving look. "Aren't you hilarious."

"My Mathadar prefers the term capricious. In all honesty we have fifty-three. I spend time with every single little warrior each day. The nursery takes up an entire wing in our home, and a full accompaniment of caretakers oversee them round the clock. I honestly don't know what we would do without them."

"The caretakers or the little ones?"

Laughing again, Queen Cassandra responded, "Both. I can tell you are going to be handful. How many do you have so far?"

"We make them one or two at a time. I like it better that way. I'd be overwhelmed with so many."

Running a finger over the little one's cheek, Cassandra mused out loud, "Ares. It's a fitting name for a warrior."

"That's what we thought."

"You can't imagine how thankful the Yuroba were that you recovered Sinthia unharmed. They have been scouring the galaxy looking for her."

"Sinthia is something else. She's a real fighter."

"I should say so—she helped us defeat a vicious Draconian queen. It was a difficult task, and more than one of us was maimed in the process. Is she among your party? I would love to speak with her."

Shaking her head, Hope explained. "She called for a Yuroba ship to treat Vxion's injuries. He was wounded in battle and didn't recover as well as we had hoped. She is convinced her people will be able to make him well again."

"I will call and check on them later this evening. How will you go about building your city?"

"We harvested right before leaving Exion, and I set aside a metric ton of resources to trade for the supplies we need. I will transfer some into Intergalactic credits and hold the rest in reserve for dark times. One never knows what the future holds."

"That is smart. I used most of our resources to ease the way for claiming this planet, getting us included in the galactic council, and luring brides for my warriors."

"You've been a busy lady."

"Honestly, time flies by for me. It seems like we only arrived yesterday, then I walk outside and see a vast modern city. It hits me that we've been building at an accelerated pace for four whole years."

"I envy you, knowing that you built a new world from the ground up."

"It is rewarding. If you like, we can meet formally tomorrow and go over the advantages of the remaining eight continents on this planet. I'm certain you will find something you like."

"Do you have any objection to our elder warriors arranging scouting expeditions?"

"Not at all. They are just large empty continents after all. We have arranged sleeping accommodations for you and your family."

"We were planning to return to our quarters on the mother ship. All our things for the little one are there."

"If you wish. We stayed in our queen suite right up until our palace was completed. Do you mind if I ask what became of the young queen Lakara?"

"We linked with an advanced medical team from Lardel One while in route to Onello. They managed to

remove the symbiont. Though the procedure was successful, it has left her weak. We expect a full recovery, but her
breeders wish nothing to do with her, and she is devastated
by the experience of being under the control of the
symbiont. She wishes to be left alone in her grief. We gathered all her possessions and created an appropriate personal
space for her to recover in. I try to visit with her a little each
day, as do several of the other women. Seeing the haunted
look in her eyes is difficult to bear."

"We have a young queen who was once host to a
symbiont. Perhaps, Queen Shanta would be willing to talk
with her."

"I would be grateful for any assistance she could give.
Queen Lakara will not even speak to her own family, for she
feels profound grief at all her symbiont put them through."

"Shanta went through a period of self-loathing as well.
It was difficult for her to accept that she was physically
unable to stop the atrocities committed by her symbiont.
Perhaps when Lakara is feeling better, things will look
differently."

"I pray that is true."

HOPE

Standing on the continent selected by the elders, Hope enjoyed the view of the rising sun from a ridge overlooking a huge flat plain. Her takadon was standing at her back with his arms wrapped snugly around her body to ward off the bite of the midwinter chill. Ares was tucked high up on her pregnant belly, with two tiny hands grasping Larok's wings. He seemed as delighted by the view as anyone else. Ares turned to look up at her and chirped happily, flapping his tiny wings. She smiled down at him. He leaned back onto her belly, and then with two tiny hands, he held on and flipped his legs over his father's locked wings. Swinging his feet, he tilted his head back and forth making some kind of sing-song noise. Grinning, she realized the little guy was humming.

"What do you think, Hope? Is our new continent to your liking?"

"It's absolutely beautiful, Larok. Your father and the rest of the elder council chose wisely."

"If so, it is only because you have taught us that at times

males have the right of choosing. I still wonder if you gave up too much control to the elder council."

"I know you trust our judgement more than theirs, but we won't always be around to see to all the details of running a government. There needs to be a good balance of power between the throne and the elder council. Perhaps in the future, a couple could land in the throne that might be less concerned with the wellbeing of everyone, or the elder council might become riddled with warriors bent on favoring their own families. A balance of power between the two is our best assurance that the will of the warriors and their families will be respected for all time."

"I can see a time when the young of our young might not have our clarity of thinking because they have only ever known freedom. Perhaps the system we devise today will keep them from turning on one another in the future."

Relaxing back against his chest, Hope sighed. "Let us not worry over future problems that might never come to pass. Today, we embark on a new age, one where Draconians and humans work together to build something worthy to be passed on to our progeny. Our elder council has served us well. I wish to raise a monument in their honor to mark the occasion. Perhaps all twenty of them carved in stone, standing in a circle with their hands joined in unity. What say you, my takadon?"

She turned to see him looking down at her with warm affection shining in his eyes. "I say that you become more queenly with each passing day. That was a speech worthy of a true Draconian queen, if ever there was one."

Hope lolled her head back against his chest, and he captured her lips in a long luxurious kiss that was only interrupted by their infuriated son. He was yammering something unintelligible and trying to pull Larok's locked wings apart. When that didn't work, he marched up Larok's arm and used his tiny foot to kick him in the top of his wing. He mumbled something else they couldn't quite understand, and his tiny horns were standing straight up. It made Hope think her little guy was truly furious. The little one promptly climbed up that very same wing and nestled himself down between the top of the startled man's upper wing base and back.

Hope commented curiously. "He's never done anything like that before. Any idea what all that was about, because I have no clue."

Larok let out an exasperated chirp. "Draconian hatchlings are high-strung and difficult to manage. I do hope you will forgive our little one for his tantrum. He apparently thinks kissing you is stealing your breath."

Choking back her shock, Hope asked, "Why in the world would he think something that strange?"

Shaking his head in annoyance, her handsome warrior responded, "How would I know? My scion speaks gibberish. I can barely make out a few mangled words. I seriously doubt he understands a word we say to him at this stage in his development."

Hope lifted both hands up over her head and ran them down Larok's neck to touch Aries. His ranting seemed to have calmed down. "The poor little guy probably wore himself out. Draconian babies are nothing like human babies."

Rubbing her belly, he purred, "Let's hope they are more reasonable."

Hope laughed. Turning in his arms, she rested her hands on his chest. "Human infants are dumb as a box of rocks for a very long time compared to Draconian babies. Don't get me wrong, they'll catch up pretty quick but the first few months they just lay there staring up at you, occasionally playing with a mobile or small toy."

Larok smiled. "Draconian young are active and inquisitive from the time they leave the incubator." He rolled his eyes, mimicking the human mannerism he thought was so useful. "They also stomp around, fly at an early age, and rummage through everything that is not sealed shut. I wouldn't exactly call them smart. They talk all the time, and no one can ever make out what they are saying."

Hope giggled at his very accurate description of his son. "They remind me so much of a mythical creature we call fairies that it makes me wonder if Draconians visited Earth in ancient times. Some of our early myths describe them as curious and precocious creatures that fly around nosing into everything. We also have stories about dragons. So, there's that as well."

"That sounds about right to me. Maybe that's why we're breed compatible. Perhaps some human DNA was mixed with ours when the first clades were formed. Speaking of breeding, you know how much I love seeing your beautiful round belly."

Hope's pregnancy hormones were making her want sex all the time, so she jumped at the chance to spend a little one-on-one time with her takadon. "What do you say about us unloading the little one on your father, and enjoying a little private celebration in honor of selecting a continent for our new settlement?"

His lips curled up into a sexy smile. "I'd say that is a very good idea. It has been too long since I sampled your queenly treasures."

Images of Larok lifting her into the air and splaying her open on his face drifted through her mind. "Yes, last night seems like forever ago, my king."

The look on his face was pure male pride tinged with a thick overlay of lust. It was a very good look for him. A feeling of utter happiness spread through Hope's entire body. This is what it felt like to get all she was ever bold enough to wish for and then some. This was her own personal happily ever after, and she intended to enjoy every single second of it.

———

Continue the Draconian story with Stacy and Meric in Alien Captain's Claimed Bride!

GLOSSARY

Akes – Draconian god of hunting, war, and violence. He is the consort to Entares, the benevolent goddess worshiped by Draconian males.

Avada – Small carrot-like vegetable that is seasoned and wrapped in a dry leaf.

Challenge –Draconian queens settle disagreements and property disputes by challenging one another in single combat. It is usually a battle to the death.

Clade – Group of Draconians who are descended from a common set of genetic code.

Doma – Type of Draconian flatbread.

Exion – Vast Sector of space encompassing the Draconian home world. Exion is ruled by a race of ruthless females bent on conquest and power.

Draconian - Were created by mixing dragon DNA with humanoid DNA. There are many family lines with unique strengths and weaknesses.

Entares – Draconian goddess of beauty, peace and joy. The males worship her as she represents their desire for females to show kindness and respect to them for their many sacrifices, rather than the harsh treatment they normally receive.

Laser Pistol –A weapon used in battles and self-defense which uses power packs to fire short laser bursts.

Naxis – Vast sector of space encompassing five galaxies, including the Milky Way.

Parsec – Unit of distance. Used mostly in determining distance in space.

Parthenogenesis – Draconians males undergo partheno-genesis when exposed to a female's pheromones. It results them incubating eggs in their bodies which are released into specially designed incubators.

Raspian – The second mother ship and one Hope and Larok use for the voyage to Onello.

Revidian – The word used by Draconians to denote a warrior performing oral sex on a queen.

Hatching – Draconian method of reproduction by which warriors conceive and carry eggs.

Hatchling – Noun: Child. Verb: Act of creating young by a male Draconian. Males hatch many times during their lifetimes.

Hatchmate – Refers to only the children hatched during the same cycle of breeding.

Strovian – Race of warriors who are at peace with the Draconians in the Naxis sector.

The Obsidian – The name of their ship.

Takadon – The Draconian word for a male who is chosen to be the queen's primary breeder. He is to stay at her side constantly and is her protector.

Taladar – Species who initiated a trade agreement with Earth to exchange much needed food and other supplies for human brides.

Tankea – Draconian word meaning love between a parent and child or between siblings.

Tricon – Unit of thickness.

Utaka Larva – Pupa stage of growth for tiny colorful flying creatures the Draconians keep for pets.

Vithacan – Symbionts that attach themselves to other creatures and survive off their emotional energy. Soul-suckers is a disrespectful term for their race.

Zelerians – Race of squid-like creatures with few humanoid features.

Made in the USA
Coppell, TX
01 June 2021

56705637R00142